Forever **ℱℬ** *Classics*

SPEAK SOFTLY, LOVE

Kathleen Yapp

Forever **Classics**

is an imprint of
Guideposts Associates, Inc.
Carmel, NY 10512

This Guideposts edition is published by special arrangement with
Kathleen Yapp.

Edited by Nancye Willis and Anne Severance
Designed by Kim Koning

Printed in the United States of America

To David, Lisa, Jim, and Terry—
precious children who have enriched my life

CHAPTER 1

Northeastern Pennsylvania—1803

GRAY CLOUDS HUNG LOW in the September sky, threatening rain, when the body of Simon Parsons was lowered to its final resting place.

Sara watched the roughly hewn pine box disappear into the ground, and even then she could not believe he was gone—this man who had been her husband for only six months.

She was surprised that the grave was so small. It looked hardly able to accommodate a child, let alone a grown man. Still, Simon was not . . . had not been . . . a large man. He had stood less than six feet by many inches and had been slight of build.

The entire community was there, in the tiny graveyard which nestled against the meeting hall. A funeral—a burying—was rare in the religious Society which had gradually come to be, over the past fifty years, as one family, then another, had settled in the fertile Alquin Valley of northeastern Pennsylvania, happy to find neighbors of like faith. Sara had been with them for all of her eighteen years.

Most of the people stood silent, although some, with hands clasped and heads bowed, prayed aloud softly. Small children clung to the hands of parents or older brothers and sisters, and tried not to gawk as the box was lowered into the ground.

Sara stood beside her husband's grave, a small childlike figure in a plain black dress. It was not a dress of mourning, but the same kind of garment she wore every day. Her hair, the color of summer wheat, was brushed away from her forehead and held in place under a black cotton bonnet which protected beneath its brim her gently curved cheeks and flawless skin.

Sara felt strangely calm. Her hands lay peacefully folded at her waist; her eyes, great circles of smoky blue, held no tears. Not even her forehead was creased in concern. But her lips, softly pink and full, were separated, and she was breathing more heavily than usual. She just couldn't stop thinking of Simon and the way he had died.

It had happened in their own bed, while she had slept peacefully beside him. Something to do with his heart, one of the elders had told her. She had awakened to find his lifeless form and she had screamed, she was ashamed to admit, and covered her face with her hands to block out the horrible sight.

Later, the elders had been very kind to her as she wept—it was permitted in her own home—and wrung her hands while sitting in a straight-backed chair, her head hanging dejectedly, great tears of guilt spilling onto the lap of the long apron that covered her dark cotton dress, making little wet splotches in the well-worn material.

"Now, now, Sister Parsons." Elder Johns had stood tall in front of her chair stroking his long, carefully brushed beard. He had used the same voice he used on the Lord's Day to speak to the congregation the words of faith. "You must not blame yourself. I'm sure the least movement from Simon would have awakened you. He simply died in his sleep."

"He was at peace," Elder Bates had said. "There was almost a smile on his lips."

"He just slipped away," Elder Jacobs confirmed.

Sara had looked up at them, tears lying gently on the silky curve of her pale cheeks, a glimmer of hope springing into her reddened eyes. "There was nothing I could have done?"

"Nothing, Sister Parsons. It was God's choosing."

Sara stepped closer to her husband's grave, remembering with pain that day of his death. She felt like a lost lamb in need of a shepherd. It had been such a short time ago that the elders had come to talk with her about marrying Simon. She remembered that time, too. There had never been, of course, any question that Simon was a good man, and would make a fine husband, but the fact that he was twenty-three years older than Sara had concerned the leaders.

Simon had been married before, but had lost his wife in childbirth. Sara had not been wife to any man and was, therefore, inexperienced in womanly ways, though she had an excellent reputation for tailoring and cooking and a talent for tending the sick and wounded. The elders had asked her if she thought she would be able to satisfy Simon's needs, both physically and spiritually. After much prayer and consideration, and after hearing Simon's persuasive argument that he needed a woman to care for his home and help him in the fields, Sara had consented to marry him. A woman her age needed a husband, she knew, and Simon was willing to have her.

She had had no idea how relieved the elders were to see her under the protection of a husband. She was an extraordinarily beautiful girl, with a winning smile and a gentle shyness that appealed to male and female alike. It had not gone unnoticed how much the men, both married and unmarried, enjoyed being around

9

the young orphan girl whose past was a mystery to them all.

Her eyes, huge and blue like a misty summer's sky, and her lips, soft and curving, gave her face an angelic appearance, and as she approached womanhood, it was apparent that Sara would soon need a husband, or there was sure to be trouble.

Simon Parsons had provided the ideal answer to the unspoken concern of the Society.

Now, Sara looked into the shallow grave and thought that life was over for her. A woman's whole existence lay in her husband, and now she had none. What was she to do? What was to be life's purpose for her? She had no children to care for, and she did not think she could do the work of the farm alone.

She shuddered as a chill breeze whipped the skirt of her dress and blew at her narrow shoulders. She lifted her eyes and looked at the people who had come to the burying. She knew them all, most of them all her life: the Jordans who worked the eighty acres next to hers and Simon's, with their two young daughters; the Swansons; the Duffs; and the MacReadys, Mrs. MacReady holding their newest child, which made ten in all. These were simple people, hard-working farmers mostly.

They were a strange mixture. Some had come from England or France in the late 1700s, to protest the domination of the church by the state, while other families had migrated from the states surrounding Pennsylvania, looking for that place which William Penn had established as an "holy experiment" on religious principles. The Alquin Valley was home, freed from ridicule and abuse—a place where one could work hard and raise one's family in peace. It was a good land, but it belonged to families, and Sara had no family.

A light rain began to fall before they finished singing the last hymn, and mothers with young children left the scene to get them inside. One by one the others slipped away, and in the end Sara stood nearly alone, looking down into the raw earth in which the remains of her husband now lay. There were no tears. She had shed them all the day she had found him dead. She stared a long time at the coffin, unaware of the chilling rain as it fell harder now and began to soak her dress.

"Come along, dear." She heard the concerned voice of Mrs. MacReady beside her even as she felt the strong hands of the woman take her shoulders and begin to pull her back from the scene of death. "You'll catch your death." A shawl was thrown about her.

Woodenly Sara allowed the older woman to lead her back to the tiny two-room house she and Simon had shared, the same house in which he had lived with his first wife. Inside, a long wooden table had been set up, now laden with many containers of food, something having been brought by each family in the Society. Sara, though grateful for their thoughtfulness, was somehow incapable of showing her proper feelings. But it didn't matter. She knew they understood and felt a particular sorrow for her because she had lost her provider.

Throughout the rest of the afternoon people came and went, assuring Sara that Simon was now with the Lord and that someday she would be reunited with him. Sara acknowledged their kind gestures with an accepting little smile that made her all the more pitiable.

The next day, alone at last, Sara cleaned the house, scrubbing with a diligence everything to be found there—the furniture, the floor, her clothes, even the few dishes she and Simon had owned. She did not question why she worked so hard; she just knew she had to have everything spotless, even though Simon was no longer there to see it.

It was decided by the elders of the Society, and Sara passively agreed, that she would move in with the MacReadys, to help with their many children and the household duties. In return she would share a small room with two teen-aged daughters, and be fed with the rest of the family, while a couple new to the Society would take over the home she had shared with Simon.

Days blended into weeks, and weeks into months. The numbness Sara had felt from losing Simon gradually diminished, to be replaced by an ungrudging acceptance of the new life that had been thrust upon her.

She began to enjoy living at the MacReadys. The children ranged in ages from three months to sixteen years. They were a noisy, happy bunch, usually good-natured, and as hard-working as their parents. Though George and Lottie MacReady sympathized with Sara over her loss, they expected her to do her share to earn her daily bread at their humble table. The constant press of the family around her reminded Sara daily that she would never have children and a husband of her own. She had vowed to herself only days after Simon's death never to marry again. The heart-rending reason behind that severe decision lay deep in Sara's soul and every now and then brought lonely tears to her sad blue eyes.

It was over a year later that Elder Johns called at the MacReady house around midday. Sara was feeding baby Eva at the time, and held her on one hip to open the door to his strong knock. She was surprised to find the elder there, and with him a beautiful older woman whom she had never seen before, and who certainly did not belong to the Society.

The stranger had very white hair, smooth fair skin, and eyes of deep green, sparkling with life. Around her shoulders was draped a long gray cloak with a high neck, for the weather was cold, and on her head was a stylish hat decorated with a lavish purple plume.

She smiled at Sara with kindness. Sara quite naturally smiled back. She had never seen a woman of such elegance in her entire life, and her mouth hung open a little in awe until she remembered her manners and invited them to step inside.

"Sister Parsons," Elder Johns said, after the door had been closed behind them to keep out the chill November air, "this lady has come a very long way to meet you."

He helped the woman remove her cloak, for the room was warm.

Sara stared at her exquisite walking dress—lavender challis, buttoned to the neck, with long sleeves puffed at the top and a narrow gored skirt trimmed with delicate lace at the bottom.

Sara found the eyes of the lovely woman upon her, examining her with the same great interest that she was showing in return.

"Mrs. Throne," Elder Johns said, "this is your brother Simon's wife, Sara. Sister Parsons, may I present Mrs. Catherine Throne, Simon's sister."

Sara's eyes widened in amazement. She had not known Simon had a sister. He had never once mentioned it to her.

"My dear child," the woman said, gently taking her hands in hers and squeezing them just a little. She was wearing gloves that were very soft. "I am so sorry about Simon's passing." She paused, noting that the girl was staring at her with a great degree of puzzlement. "I can see he never mentioned me to you, did he?" She released Sara's hands.

"No, ma'am," Sara said softly.

"I thought not. When Simon joined the Society, he made it very clear that he wanted no more contact with the outside world. And that included me."

"Why?" Sara blurted. What a rude question that had been, she suddenly realized.

"It's a long story," Mrs. Throne replied wistfully. "Perhaps I shall tell it to you one day." She smiled warmly. "I must admit, Sara, that I was surprised to learn that Simon had taken so young a wife. But now that I see you, I can understand why he would have done so. You are very beautiful."

"Spiritual beauty is to be desired more than physical beauty," intoned Elder Johns.

Mrs. Throne nodded her head in agreement. "Indeed, it is. I, too, am a religious person, and I can discern that Sara's greater beauty comes from within."

"My dear," she continued, "after I received word of Simon's death from Elder Johns, I waited a year before coming to meet you, so that the proper mourning period could be observed. Now that it is over, I would be very pleased if you would consent to return with me to my home in Virginia. It would be good for both of us to become better acquainted. I'd like to learn of my brother's life here, and you would probably like to know something of his younger days. Simon was a difficult man to understand, but I loved him dearly. We were very close when we were growing up. I never quite got over his leaving home. . . . Oh, Sara, please say you'll come. We could console each other in our loss."

The urgent plea in Mrs. Throne's voice and in her eyes persuaded Sara to accept. *Maybe it would be a good thing*, she thought. A kindlier woman she had never met, and it would be interesting to learn about Simon's earlier life, of which he had never spoken.

"I'd be happy to come for a visit, Mrs. Throne, if it is permitted, that is." She looked warily at Elder Johns. "But my place is here with the Society of course. I have responsibilities to the family with whom I'm now living, and I couldn't possibly leave them for long."

14

"I've spoken to George MacReady, Sister Parsons," Elder Johns confirmed with a nod, "and he's agreed to let you go for a while, if you would like to do so."

"Really?" Sara's eyes shone with an unexpected excitement. "Then I shall be very pleased to accompany you, Mrs. Throne,"—remembering her obligation, she sobered—"for a short visit." She lowered her eyes demurely, repressing the unseemly exuberance she felt.

"Oh, my dear! You cannot know how this decision pleases me. And I shall bring you back whenever you like."

Sara looked eagerly to Elder Johns. "It's really all right that I go?"

"Yes, Sister Parsons, it is. Mrs. Throne is your only family—now that Simon's gone."

She risked a small smile. "Then I should be getting ready. The sooner I leave, the sooner I can be returning to my duties. The MacReadys have so many children and there is so much to do . . . you understand, I hope."

"Of course, my dear, and your sense of loyalty is commendable. Now that it's settled, let me say that I have a carriage waiting. Would you like some help with your packing?"

Reminded of her skimpy wardrobe, Sara spoke hastily. "Oh, no ma'am. It will take only a few minutes. Perhaps you would like some tea while you wait."

"Yes, thank you. That would be delightful."

Catherine Throne sat in a hard chair by the fireplace, and Elder Johns went his way, while Sara moved quietly about the room preparing the tea, using water from a cast-iron kettle that hung over the fire. She dared not give way to the exhilaration that suddenly seized her and threatened to spill over, sending her fairly flying from the room to gather her

15

few possessions. Why, she had never been outside the Society in her entire life—or, at least, for as long as she could remember. And the very thought of it both terrified and intrigued her.

CHAPTER 2

CATHERINE THRONE LIVED AT THE OUTSKIRTS of a lovely
little town called Charlottesville, located in the central
part of the state of Virginia and nestled in an immense
natural bowl in the foothills of the Blue Ridge
Mountains.

Grand Oak was like nothing Sara could ever have
imagined. English Georgian in style of architecture,
and square in shape, it had two stories with elaborate
brickwork on the outside, and ornamental cornices
decorating the edges of the roof. Inside, the downstairs was built around a central hall with two large
rooms on either side and a wide intricately carved
mahogany staircase rising at the end of the hall to the
second floor where the bedrooms were located.

Sara had a room all to herself, which amazed her,
and frightened her as well. Always before she had
shared one, either with the family that raised her, or
with Simon, or with the MacReady children. Now she
was alone, and it would take some getting used to.
Her bedroom was tastefully and expensively decorated in varying shades of green, and Sara wondered

what it would be like to live one's entire life surrounded by such magnificence.

The first thing one noticed when entering the room was the impressive bed. Its tall posts at each corner supported a short canopy from which hung exquisite brocade curtains. Lying on the bed was pure heaven, for the mattress was stuffed with feathers and rested on woven ropes fastened to the bedstead several feet above the floor. How different from her mattress in the MacReady house, which was a canvas bag stuffed with straw and placed on the floor.

The downstairs dining room and parlors—there were two: one for ladies and another for gentlemen—were elegantly paneled with smooth wood and furnished with finely designed tables and chairs and sofas. Catherine mentioned names like Chippendale, Hepplewhite, Sheraton, and the Adams brothers, none of which meant anything to Sara, but whom she understood, nonetheless, to be among the finest craftsmen of that day.

For the first few days of her visit with Catherine, Sara wandered happily from room to room examining everything carefully, noting the muted colors, admiring the patina of the woods, appreciating the warmth of the carpets on the floor and the heat emanating from the large and impressive fireplaces, which were the focal points in each room.

Catherine was a kind and generous hostess, doing everything she could to ensure Sara's comfort. She had the cook prepare some of Sara's favorite foods, and introduced her to several new delicacies.

The conversation centered often around Simon.

"Simon was never easy to understand," Catherine told Sara. "Even as a young boy he was restless, rather unyielding, always searching for something to bring him peace. Nothing ever did. He fought with our father constantly and I, unfortunately, was often

18

caught in the middle, trying to see both sides, reconciling the two."

"Was he unhappy at home?" Sara asked.

"I would have to say yes. He never quite fit in." Catherine sighed and sat back on a chair upholstered in silk damask. They were in the ladies' parlor, having tea. It was late afternoon now, and the sun had left the sky. The light in the room was growing dimmer, and the fire needed to be stoked. But both women were lost in a reverie of thought—one, remembering things that had happened long ago; the other, struggling to focus new pictures of a dead husband she had never truly known.

"Our father was a wealthy gentleman farmer," Catherine explained. "For some reason, Simon always resented the fact. Perhaps it was because Father expected him to carry on the family business. But Simon wanted none of it. He read a great deal, lost in a world of his own making. He cared nothing for the land or the crops that bought us expensive clothes and a grand home and money with which to entertain lavishly and take trips. He much preferred to be by himself, studying some dusty book most people had never heard of."

"But he was a farmer in the Society," Sara observed.

"Yes, that *is* strange, isn't it?" she mused.

"Why did Simon leave home?"

Catherine studied Sara for several moments before answering. "He and I had a serious quarrel. He was very angry with me. It was a good excuse for him to do what he had always wanted to do—run away to another life. I never saw him again, although I did have one letter from him, years after he joined the Society. He said he had found his place. He sounded happy and contented. At last."

Sara wanted to ask about the quarrel that had prompted Simon's leaving home, but she sensed

Catherine did not want to tell her. Perhaps it was something better not resurrected. If so, the secret would lie buried with Simon.

"I'm anxious to meet your daughter Lydia," Sara said, hoping the change of subject would erase the fine lines of distress etched across Catherine's forehead. "When does she arrive home from Charleston?"

"In a few days. I hope the two of you will get along, but I should warn you that Lydia is a handful. She's high-spirited—spoiled, I blush to admit. She may be difficult to get to know, Sara. Your background is so different from her own—and Lydia is not very tolerant, I'm afraid." The apology in her voice affected Sara deeply. To have known such a mother's love to her seemed the ultimate joy. Was there some rift between them?

"I understand." Though of course, she didn't.

Catherine's smile was wan. "I hope you'll still be able to say that after you've met Lydia. If I could just see her married . . . perhaps a good husband would tame her a bit."

After dinner Catherine excused herself, saying she had some letters to write, and Sara went into the library with every intention of working on a miniature tapestry she hoped to frame and give to her hostess in appreciation of her hospitality. But once she sat down in the comfortable wing-backed chair and relaxed, she found her mind entertaining all sorts of disturbing thoughts.

In addition to the confusing picture Catherine Throne had painted of her daughter Lydia, Sara was concerned that she herself was becoming worldly-minded. She knew she was enjoying far too much the lifestyle Catherine Throne had introduced to her. The bed in which she was sleeping was more comfortable than anything she had ever slept on before. The sheets and handmade quilts were of fine soft material she loved to touch. The rug on the floor in her room welcomed her bare feet. The intricately carved high-boy in which her few paltry articles of clothing were stored was lovely to behold. The list went on.

Sara was aware of every minute detail in Catherine's house—from the exquisite English silverware and Waterford crystal used at each meal to the lovely pieces of Chinese porcelain that decorated tables and shelves throughout the house. The delicious food, the abundance of clothing which hung in Catherine's and Lydia's armoires, the cluster of servants who graciously fulfilled any need she might have—all combined to make Sara feel like a pampered princess. And, at the moment, a princess plagued by guilt.

In the few days she had been a guest at Grand Oak, her mind had not stopped recording all the luxuries. It was not that she was envious or covetous of the things Catherine possessed, or that she begrudged her the fruits of her and her husband's labors. Mr. Throne had been an architect in Charlottesville, the county seat, and had been very successful in his trade before his death eight years before. But to have so much when others had so little caused Sara to ponder why it should be so. She thought in particular about the MacReadys, with their ten children, crowded into a humble little home with only a few tiny rooms. Was that the way God intended His people to live? Did He disapprove of material success such as Catherine enjoyed, or was He honoring her for her devotion to Him?

Sara could not help wondering what it would be like to be the mistress of a house like this. On the one hand, of course, to a simple farm girl like herself, accustomed to only the bare necessities of life, it seemed an awesome responsibility. There were so very many "things" to be cared for. At the same time the advantages were readily clear—never to have another worry about money, to be attended by servants day and night, to be able to buy whatever your heart fancied. Would she tire of all that after a while? Would such easy access to whatever pleasures she desired eventually warp her spiritual commitment by becoming a stronger god than the God she now served?

She was wise enough to know that having many possessions, as Catherine did, might lead a person of weak character into the temptation of putting trust in them rather than in the Lord's provision.

Sara decided she was better off with the Society, with people who asked little from life other than the freedom to worship as they chose, health to do a full day's work, and the privilege of providing for their families. She knew she'd rather have the knowledge of God and His presence in her life than all the silver and gold the world could offer.

Seeing a copy of the Bible on one of the nearby tables, Sara put aside her sewing and went over and picked it up. She opened the Holy Book to a favorite passage in the New Testament, sat back down, and began to read the words aloud, pondering them as she did so, a look of deep contemplation wreathing her face in a beautiful expression. She did not notice the two people standing in the doorway, watching her.

"Sara, there is someone here I would like you to meet."

Startled, Sara looked up to see Catherine sweeping into the room, her arm resting on that of a young man—a tall, handsome man of aristocratic bearing and dressed in elegant clothes.

"Sara," Catherine said, smiling broadly, "may I present Dominic Lansford. Dominic, this is our Sara."

Slowly Sara rose from the chair, still holding the Bible in her hands, her eyes and lips smiling a welcome.

His eyes were very blue, his hair black and thick.

He was even taller close up, and lean, but well-built beneath his expensive and fashionable clothing.

"And she is every bit as pious as you said she was, Catherine," he said, without taking his eyes from Sara's face, his lips smiling in a way that made Sara feel he was mocking her.

"Sara is an unusual girl, Dominic, as I am sure you will learn," Catherine answered him.

"I can see that already," he said, and he held out his hand toward Sara, but she did not know why. She stood looking at him and then he reached for her hand and slowly raised it by the fingers to his lips, glancing down at it for a moment before kissing it so delicately that Sara did not actually feel the featherlight touch on her skin.

Whatever is he doing? she wondered, even as he released her fingers and stood erect to gaze at her face.

"Sara, Dominic is a neighbor of ours. I asked him to come by so that you could meet him."

"I see," Sara replied, with a little smile.

"I wanted you to get to know Dominic so that he could be your friend while you're here."

"Do I need a friend?" Sara asked innocently.

Dominic laughed heartily. "An honest woman who speaks her mind," he quipped. "Unique."

Catherine cleared her throat. "Shall we sit down?" she suggested.

Sara was relieved to return to her chair.

She wondered how long Catherine had known Dominic Lansford, for the older woman certainly seemed fond of him. Sara listened to the two of them as they caught up on the day's events in town and elsewhere, secretly welcoming the chance to examine this stranger at closer range.

He was a very attractive man, probably in his early thirties, with a strong face and bright intelligent eyes. His dark blue cutaway coat with black buttons was

23

worn over a gray waistcoat. Long gray skintight pantaloons disappeared into black Hessian boots. The starched white stock at his throat was carefully folded and wound around the collar until it just touched the tip of his chin. His hair, black and gleaming, was brushed forward over his forehead and his ears, the queue tied loosely in back.

Though his clothes were meticulous, he did not seem at all conscious of them. He had, instead, a natural air of masculinity, a definitive sense of self-confidence that showed itself in every aspect of his behavior, from the way in which he sat on the sofa, to the way he moved his hands. Sara especially noticed his hands. They were strong and expressive in their gesturing.

Sara felt a surge of respect for Catherine as she listened to her express her views on many different topics. How unlike the women of the Society, who would never have ventured an opinion about politics and world affairs, nor would they have been expected to do so. But Dominic encouraged Catherine's comments, even when they differed from his own. At times he laughed, his eyes sparkling with an appealing humor. But at other times he disagreed so strongly with Catherine that Sara feared their conversation would erupt into a royal argument.

Nevertheless, they continued their good-natured sparring, taunting each other, joking, agreeing and disagreeing—all in the best of spirits.

"And what is your opinion of our illustrious president, Thomas Jefferson?" Dominic asked Sara.

Sara was startled out of her contemplation. "I . . . I'm afraid I don't know enough about him to suggest a proper opinion," she replied honestly.

"And what about the Louisiana Purchase?"

"I have not heard of it. Perhaps you could enlighten me."

"Hmmm." Dominic folded his hands together in a

24

thoughtful pose and studied the girl before him. Sara felt uncomfortable with his eyes on her, embarrassed by her ignorance. She had never thought it important to think about such things, but now she wished she had.

"Sara lives with a group of people who feel there are other things more important than politics and gossip." Catherine explained Sara's vulnerability and her inability to respond to Dominic's inquiries.

"And what might those things be?" Dominic addressed his question to Sara.

Sara didn't like having to defend the Society against the unsympathetic probing of this gentleman. She would have preferred to gather up her possessions and move upstairs to her room, leaving Mr. Lansford and Catherine to discuss world events to their hearts' content. But she had been asked a question, and she supposed she should answer it before she left him.

"Let me rephrase my question," Dominic interrupted her thinking, "as I do know something about the ways of the Society. What I would like to know, instead, is how you came to be a part of that group."

Sara glanced at Catherine who nodded her head in encouragement.

"I was left there as a baby," she began, nervous under Dominic Lansford's intense scrutiny. "My father stumbled into the small settlement one day, bleeding from a gunshot wound. He was clutching me to him, but was barely able to stand on his feet. The elders took care of me and tended his wounds. When he was well enough to travel, my father left a few coins with the elders for my care, and said he would be back as soon as he concluded some business."

She stopped as a well of tears flooded into her eyes. She had not thought of this story for a long time, and was amazed at the pain she felt in recounting it.

"And what happened?" Dominic Lansford prodded.

Beneath lashes wet with emotion, Sara looked up at him, relieved to find an expression of sympathy on his face.

"He never returned."

"He abandoned you?"

"Certainly not!" The reply was tart, and irritation sparked Sara's normally serene blue eyes. Dominic raised one eyebrow in surprise. "The elders believed that he died in some way," she went on quickly. "They assured me he was most concerned for my welfare and held me tenderly in his arms before he went away."

Her eyes, once more became huge blue pools of tranquility and Dominic's sympathetic look turned hard, the muscle in his jaw flexing strangely. "So you were raised by strangers?"

"Yes, although I've never felt that way about them. The Society is my home. They are fine loving people."

"Who know nothing about what is going on in the world."

"The men do."

"And the women?"

"We know what we need to know. Besides, there are more important things to concern oneself with."

"Such as?"

"Such as striving to please God, which is the most important thing any person can do."

"That is certainly true," Catherine agreed.

"And working hard to produce food and the necessities for our families," Sara continued defensively.

The man smiled. "And did you have enough of the necessities of life, Sara?" There was a mocking tone in his voice.

"I have always had something to eat, a roof over my head, and work to keep me busy."

"And what about pleasure?"

Sara felt a rush of color converge upon her neck and cheeks. She did not like the questions this man was asking. Why did he want to know so much about her? Why didn't Catherine stop him?

"I have known many moments of pleasure in my life, Mr. Lansford." Sara answered him forthrightly, but wished she did not have to look at him and see those piercing eyes upon her. "I have not been unhappy."

"I dare say you have not been fulfilled, either."

Sara's eyes widened. "What do you mean by that?"

"Love, Sara. Have you ever been in love?"

Sara's mouth dropped open and she could not bring herself to think of an answer to such a personal question. Besides, she admitted hastily to herself, she was not at all sure what kind of love he was talking about.

"Were you happy in your marriage to Simon Parsons?" Dominic pursued the matter relentlessly.

"Of course."

"Why?"

"Why? I don't understand what you mean. Simon was my husband for only six months, but he was a good and upright man and—and I was fortunate to have him to look out for me."

"And how did the two of you—he, a man much older—decide to marry?" The eyes probed her very being, and Sara shifted restlessly in her chair. She did not want to answer him. He was a stranger, not someone to whom she owed explanations.

She fingered the rough texture of the Bible lying in her lap, taking some comfort in knowing that God was with her, and struggled to find the words to explain her way of life to this rudely curious man.

"Simon asked to marry me," she answered finally in a soft voice. "The elders thought about it and prayed over it and decided it would be a good marriage."

"Did they consult you?"

"Yes."

"Did they ask your opinion, your desires, or did they just inform you that you should marry Simon Parsons?"

"Why are you making it sound wrong for them to have done so?" Sara questioned. "It was the proper thing to do. I was of marriageable age. Simon needed a wife."

"How convenient for you both." His derisive tone rang through the room. "What about love?"

He threw the question at her and leaned forward on the sofa as he did so, his look penetrating the thin wall of self-confidence that Sara possessed.

"What do you mean—'love'?" Sara's voice trembled.

"Merciful heavens!" Dominic leaped to his feet in agitation, coming to her side and leaning down until his face was only inches from her own. "I'm talking about those very special feelings between a man and a woman that tells each of them they cannot live without the other. I'm talking about emotion, feeling, caring. Don't you understand those things at all?"

Sara was stunned into silence.

"Dominic," Catherine rose to her feet in dismissal, "I think you've asked Sara quite enough questions for tonight."

Dominic stood up straight, and adjusted the white stock at his throat. "I'm sorry," he murmured. "Please forgive my outburst." He did not look at Sara.

Rather, in leaving he addressed Catherine. "You were right in asking me to come. Sara is an unusual girl, and it has been my pleasure to meet her."

Catherine laid a hand gently on his arm. "Thank you, Dominic. We'll talk more at another time."

28

Dominic turned again to Sara who had risen shakily from her chair, uneasy and puzzled by the explosive emotion she had incited in him.

"Mrs. Parsons," he said in a more gentle tone, and his eyes were gentle, too, "I'd like to see more of you, if you would allow me the privilege. May I call on you tomorrow morning? It would give me great pleasure to show Charlottesville to you."

Sara gaped at him, shocked by his invitation. Then she looked to Catherine.

"It would do you good to get out, Sara dear," Catherine encouraged her. "You haven't left the house since you arrived. And I trust Dominic to take good care of you."

Sara hesitantly agreed, more for Catherine's sake than for her own. But she was mystified as to why Dominic Lansford should want to have anything at all to do with her.

CHAPTER 3

CATHERINE INSISTED SARA WEAR ONE of Lydia's dresses for her walk with Dominic the next morning. Sara tried to refuse but sensed that Catherine did not want her to be embarrassed on the streets of Charlottesville, clad in her simple farm clothes, while Dominic was attired in the very latest European fashion. So, she allowed Catherine to select something appropriate.

The woman Sara became under Catherine's deft touch stared back at her from the full-length mirror, eyes wide in wonder. Was that enchanting creature really Sara Parsons? The pale lavender velvet walking dress, with its high-waisted bodice and long sleeves, brought a rosy glow to cheeks she had always assumed were ruddy from too much exposure to the sun. And there seemed to be warm sapphire lights sparkling in her eyes!

Sara was amazed, too, at the transformation in her figure. Never had she owned a dress that hugged her so tightly, lifting her shapely bosom, then flowing in elegant folds to a narrow ruffle at the hemline. To see herself in this way made her blush. She wondered what Dominic would think. It seemed improper, even unwise, to appear in such a garment. But surely Catherine knew best in such matters.

Catherine supervised the curling of Sara's hair so that it peeked out from beneath a flat wide-brimmed felt hat, tied with ribbons beneath her chin. Very delicate low-heeled shoes, laced across the instep and over the ankle, matched the gown in color. Though they were a trifle large, they were nonetheless quite serviceable.

When Dominic's arrival was announced, Catherine went to greet him. Sara promised to be along soon. She needed a few moments of privacy to adjust to the beautiful stranger she had become and to gather her courage. Then she descended the stairs and stepped into the parlor.

Upon seeing Dominic, Sara's breath caught in her throat. He looked elegantly handsome in fawn-colored cashmere breeches, a brown flannel vest beneath a darker chestnut brown coat, a neckcloth of fine muslin, and a lightweight top hat edged with a narrow braid of silk. He carried a walking stick and his feet were encased in soft riding boots.

Sara walked slowly toward him, apprehensive that he would not like the way she looked, afraid he would think her presumptuous for borrowing one of Lydia's dresses, even though it had been at Catherine's suggestion.

Engaged in conversation with Catherine, Dominic's eyes caught her movement, and he turned to regard her, eyebrows lifted in stunned surprise.

Sara scarcely breathed, feeling certain he would not approve of her trying to be someone she was not. She knew she should be wearing simple linen, not expensive velvet. She was not a well-bred young lady. She was a farm girl.

Dominic stepped up to her and captured her gaze. "You look ravishing this morning, Sara." His compli-

31

ment, uttered in rich and well-modulated tones, was an utter surprise to Sara. "I'm afraid to take you out on the streets for fear you'll be snatched away by some admirer who will be overwhelmed by your beauty."

He held out his hand to her. This time Sara knew to put her own into it. He raised her fingers to his lips, looking at her all the while, as though not wanting to miss for a moment the chance to see her.

Sara trembled.

"Shall we go?" he suggested, and Catherine wished them a good morning as they walked through the wide double doors and out into the sunshine.

In descending the steps of the veranda, Dominic's hand lightly supported Sara's elbow. She was acutely aware of his touch—thrilled by it, in fact, but guilt-ridden as well. In the Society, men and women who were not married to each other never touched. Such license was strictly forbidden.

To her dismay, Sara realized that she liked Dominic's touch, and even though she knew she should not allow it, she justified it by telling herself that Charlottesville was a different world from that of the Society in the Alquin Valley. Dominic was not being forward by taking her arm, only solicitous of her as a proper gentleman should be, and so she tried to relax. But she wondered if he sensed her nervousness, brought on simply by his nearness.

It was a typical November day. The sun was shining, as it almost always was—"Even in winter," Dominic said—but despite its brilliance, it gave little warmth. The air was crisp. They walked along the wooden sidewalks, Dominic greeting the townspeople and explaining to Sara facts about every store and building they passed.

"Charlottesville was named for Queen Charlotte, the wife of George III of England," he told her.

"I see." That was her response to just about

everything Dominic told her. *I see*. Once she had simply murmured, "Oh."

Sara knew he must think her a dolt, but she couldn't help it. She had never been alone with a man like this, even in public, and she was acutely unsure of herself. She wanted desperately to be more articulate, to prove to Dominic that she did have a brain that functioned and a mouth that could utter more than two words at a time. But it was not to be. Her mind was hopelessly mired in a mental bog, it appeared.

"It's a friendly little town, don't you think?" Dominic asked, tipping his hat to some stout matrons who were passing them and staring with undisguised interest at the stranger on his arm.

"Yes," she agreed, though to herself she fretted, *except for the young women who stopped to chat with you and practically ignored me*. She had seen in their eyes unmistakable admiration for the tall, impeccably dressed gentleman who was protectively holding her arm, as well as envy that it was she, and not they, at his side.

When the morning ended with Dominic saying he had business in another town, Sara was both sad and greatly relieved. He escorted her back to Grand Oak and, before departing, bowed courteously to her and to Catherine.

"I would be honored, Sara, if you would allow me to show you the countryside tomorrow. I have a comfortable carriage and there is much to see hereabouts that I think would interest you."

Flushing with pleasure that Dominic wanted to see her again, Sara nodded her head in agreement and murmured a "thank you" for the morning's tour.

Later, Catherine commented, "I take it you enjoyed your walk."

"Oh, yes, very much. Dominic gave me a complete history of the town of Charlottesville and pointed out interesting people and places."

"Whom did you meet?"

Sara gave her as many names as she could remember, most of them feminine.

Catherine smiled. "Ah yes. Well, you'll soon see, my dear, that Dominic is the most popular man around. Of course, the fact that he's still unmarried has much to do with that. Every unattached girl in three counties has been trying to lead him to the marriage altar for years."

"Why hasn't one of them succeeded?"

"I don't know. He certainly enjoys the company of women and is, so I am told, quite romantic. Perhaps it's that old excuse of not having found the *right* girl."

During the rest of the day Sara pondered Dominic Lansford's single state. She thought it strange that a man his age—he was thirty-one, she learned—had not taken a wife. Perhaps Dominic was the kind of man who was not content with just one adoring female and craved variety. If so, she had only heard of such men out in the world. None had ever entered her peaceful existence with the Society, and the thought that Dominic might be one of them filled her with a curious speculation.

Perhaps because of the perverse turn of her thoughts, she found herself praying rather more fervently than usual that day. Knowing that she had a Heavenly Father who was always there to listen to her deepest needs somehow compensated for the fact that she had no earthly father to whom she could turn. As Sara prayed over her walk with God, she included the names of the two new people who had suddenly become so important to her.

Dear Lord, somehow make me a blessing to Catherine and to Dominic. Catherine worships You, I know, but I'm not sure about Dominic. Let me be Your witness, and save me from my own foolish imaginings. . . .

The next morning Catherine selected a lovely blue brocade from Lydia's wardrobe for Sara to wear on her outing with Dominic.

"It makes your eyes bluer than ever," she complimented Sara.

Sara gave her a hug and twirled around the room, delighting in the luxurious feel of the fabric and wondering if Lydia really appreciated the beautiful clothes she had in abundance.

Dominic's carriage was far more than just comfortable, as he had modestly declared. Sara ran her hand along the finely upholstered leather seats, and let her fingers trail into the richly carved wooden sides. Even the coal-black horses were dashing in their harnesses decorated with silver ornaments. Because of Sara's obvious interest in them, Dominic told her he bred and raced fine quarter horses and thoroughbreds.

"Are they much different from the farm horses we have in Pennsylvania?" Sara asked.

Dominic suppressed a smile. "Quite different. Those animals are mainly for hauling heavy loads. The thoroughbred and quarter horse have been carefully trained for riding and racing. In fact, Virginians pride themselves on having developed the best saddle and racing horses in the colonies, much preferred to the walking, trotting, and cantering horses of the North. If you're really interested, Sara, I'd be happy to show you my stables some time," Dominic offered.

"I'd love to see them," Sara responded with delight.

"Then you shall, at first opportunity."

He drove with a leisurely pace throughout the hills and valleys surrounding Charlottesville, and regaled Sara with story after story of the development of the area, giving her information about the current residents as well.

"I can hardly believe that the president of the United States has a home near here!" Sara exclaimed in awe.

"What is the name of his house?"

Dominic had been quizzing her on the things he had told her, and Sara loved it. Her mind was more relaxed today and more readily absorbed the names and dates that Dominic supplied in abundance.

"Monticello," she answered confidently. "It's an Italian word that means 'little mountain.'"

"Because?"

Sara's impressively large eyes danced. "Because it is built on a mountaintop that provides a magnificent view which has inspired Mr. Jefferson since childhood." Sara became thoughtful. "How do you know that the president feels that way, Dominic?"

He threw her a sly grin and flicked the reins of the horses to speed them on their way, but said nothing.

Sara squirmed in the seat so she could look directly at her handsome guide. "Don't tell me you know Thomas Jefferson *personally*."

Dominic shrugged. "Then I shan't."

Sara gasped in amazement. "But you do, don't you? Would there ever be a way I could see Monticello, and meet Mr. Jefferson?" she asked timidly.

Dominic glanced at her from the corner of one eye. "There might be."

"Oh, Dominic!" In her exuberance she clutched his arm with both her hands. But when she realized her impropriety, she reddened to a deep scarlet and jerked her hands away and was not able to meet his amused gaze.

They were driving along a pretty country lane with tall stately blackgum trees stretching their naked limbs and branches to the sky on either side of the road when Dominic said seriously, "You have an exceptional mind, Sara Parsons, which you have not been encouraged to use. Your life is wasted in the Society."

Sara's heart thudded at the unaccustomed praise, and she dug her hands deeper into Lydia's fur muff. No one had ever spoken of her intelligence before. At

36

the same time, however, she felt a little disappointed in the Society. Dominic was right—they did not encourage women to use their minds for anything other than what was of value to their roles as wives and mothers. Within those narrow confines, the man was in charge of the barn and the outside world, while the woman's domain was house and children.

She glanced surreptitiously at him, secretly cherishing this moment of discovery. He actually seemed to enjoy discussing things with her—as he did Catherine. At the moment Dominic was looking straight ahead, his eyes on the road, his hands holding lightly the reins of the well-disciplined horses that drew their carriage.

"Do you enjoy learning?" he asked, as though he had divined her thoughts. He turned his head toward her and caught her gaze. Quickly she looked away.

"Yes, I do," she answered him truthfully. "I'm enjoying it very much."

He smiled a little. "Good. Then with your permission, I'd like to propose a program of study. I'll write out a list of books I think you should read. Catherine has them in her library. When you've finished, perhaps we can discuss your opinion of them."

"All right," Sara replied eagerly, grateful for his willingness to tutor her.

"In time," he went on, "there are people you should meet and talk with, places you should see."

Sara frowned even in her excitement. It sounded as though Dominic expected her to be around for a long time. Yet she knew she had to return soon to the Society. Her visit must not be prolonged—the Mac-Readys, with their many children and busy household, needed her.

Sara considered reminding Dominic, but hated to spoil the pleasant mood which had surrounded them all morning. She wanted to read the books he had promised to suggest to her, and to talk with him about them. She would not be missed for a few more days, she reasoned.

"I'll appreciate your help," she said shyly, "though my reading is not very fast, I'm afraid."

"It will be before I'm finished with you," he assured her, the determined set of his mouth announcing as strongly as any words that his predictions would, indeed, come about. Nor did it occur to Sara to doubt him for a moment, though she felt both pleased and embarrassed by this display of interest in her personal improvement.

Sara turned her attention to the scenery around them. To her right were rolling fields of clover, alfalfa, and succulent lespedeza, enclosed and cross-divided by white board fences that stretched on as far as the eye could see. The slim silhouettes of horses were seen from time to time, and Sara was curious to know what the place was and to whom it belonged. She asked Dominic.

."It's called 'The Willows.' "

"It's lovely!" Sara exclaimed, craning her neck to see more.

"The finest horses in Virginia, or anywhere else, for that matter, are raised there."

"Surely not finer than yours?"

"They *are* mine."

Sara gasped. "This . . . this is your . . . land?"

Dominic chuckled. "My plantation, yes."

"But there's so much of it."

"Three thousand acres of prime pasturage."

Sara stared through the fence at the land which dipped and swelled for miles in every direction. She could not begin to fathom so large a piece of land belonging to one family. She thought about the eighty acres she and Simon had farmed in Pennsylvania.

"And does your family live there with you?" she asked him. Catherine had not mentioned anything to her about his mother or father, brothers or sisters.

Dominic pulled back on the reins, slowing the

horses to an easy walk. Without looking at her, he answered indirectly, "Mine is an old family—been in this country since The Berkeley Company landed at the James River on December 4, 1619. One of the women on board their forty-ton ship, the *Margaret,* was my ancestress. She was widowed shortly after arriving here, and later married a man who was a skilled craftsman—a carpenter. Fortunately they moved away from the Berkeley settlement before it was wiped out by an Indian uprising in the spring of 1622. I still own two pieces of the man's furniture—a dining table and a small but exquisite chest."

"I'm sure you treasure them. And have all your ancestors been carpenters?"

"No. They've been a mixed bunch. Everything from gentlemen farmers to town mayors to preachers."

"Preachers? Really?"

"That's right. The present Lansford, however, is far from being a preacher." His mouth tightened a little.

"Oh?" *There.* She was doing it again—indulging in inane remarks. He would think she had learned nothing at all of polite conversation. She hurried on, "And why do you say that?"

Dominic didn't answer right away, and the gentle clip-clop of the horses' hooves on the dry hard ground was the only sound that broke the lovely pastoral silence around them.

"Let's just say he's lost a lot of the faith of his forefathers."

"How sad," Sara answered sincerely, noticing that Dominic was frowning. Talking about faith in God displeased him, and she wondered why. Wanting to restore the bright mood of their ride, Sara said, "Do you enjoy raising race horses?"

"Yes, indeed. It began as a hobby but quickly turned into a profit-making venture."

"I've never seen a race."

39

Dominic glanced at her. "If you stay long enough with Catherine, you just might."

"Do you think so?" Sara could not suppress her excitement despite the fact that there was very likely to be gambling, and she was unequivocally opposed to gambling. "They must be marvelous animals, your thoroughbreds and quarter horses, to take up all your time as they do."

Dominic's gaze deepened and his mouth moved into a grin. "They don't take *all* my time, Sara, because a horse cannot satisfy all of a man's needs."

Sara blushed from ear to ear. "I . . . I just m—meant . . ."

"I know what you meant," he said gently, "and someday, when I take you to The Willows, you'll see for yourself just how marvelous my animals are."

He studied her thoughtfully for a moment. "Would you like to ride while you're visiting Catherine? You could come over whenever you like."

Dominic's offer surprised Sara. To be allowed to ride one of his horses would be an honor. It would also mean she'd see him more often, which pleased and frightened her equally.

"I might not be able to handle such a fine horse," she admitted candidly. "I'm used to pokey ones that pull a plow."

"I'll teach you. Do you have the proper attire?"

Sara had no idea what the proper attire was, but before she could reply, Dominic added, "I'll talk to Catherine about it. But now, I want to ask you a very serious question." He reined in the horses and turned to look at her, placing his arm along the back of the seat, his hand resting dangerously near her shoulder.

"What do you want from life, little Sara?"

His questioning gaze traveled leisurely over her face, and Sara was not sure whether the sudden warmth that flamed her cheeks came because she did not know how to answer his question or because his dark searching eyes were dwelling on her so intently.

He did not press her for an answer, and the seconds blended into long moments of silence in which Sara grappled with what she might say.

"I suppose . . . I want to be at peace, with myself, and the world around me, and . . . to know that I am doing God's will."

Dominic frowned. "What is God's will for you, Sara? Does He want you to spend the rest of your life buried in that lonely Pennsylvania valley, caring for someone else's children and home?"

His hand moved up and caressed her cheek. "Or are you going to be given again in marriage to an old man who will never be able to fully appreciate you?"

His eyes lingered on her hair, then on her full pink lips, now parted. "Will you ever know the kind of love that could be yours . . . somewhere else?"

He kissed her very gently and his hand came to rest on her shoulder.

He lifted his head and Sara gazed at him in wonder.

"My little Sara," he said softly, "there is so much about the world that you have yet to learn. I would like to teach you. You must come to The Willows. There are some things there I think will interest you."

"Yes, I would like that," she whispered, mesmerized. "I'd like to meet your parents, your family."

The mouth that only moments before had caressed her lips drew into a hard line and he straightened in the seat. He turned his eyes straight ahead.

"I have no family." He flicked the reins of the horses, and the moment of tenderness they had shared vanished.

All the way back to Grand Oak, Dominic did not speak to Sara, and she was miserable, knowing her innocent remark had angered him and ruined their outing. But why?

Sara could not forget how it had felt to have Dominic's mouth on hers. Her lips burned with the imprint of his kiss. It had been a chaste one, light and momentary, much like a fond peck a brother would

41

give to a sister—no doubt, the way he had intended it. Of course, Dominic should not have kissed her at all! It had been a brazen thing to do—she, a widow—even if it was only a friendly kiss. It was insulting. It was disrespectful.

Still, it had been wonderful and warm and exciting, hinting at that kind of love Dominic had implied would probably never be hers if she returned to the Society. But there was no question she *would* return.

Back at Grand Oak, Dominic helped Sara alight from the carriage, his hand supporting her as she descended.

In silence they started up the stairs to the veranda which ran across the front of the house. Suddenly Dominic took Sara by both shoulders and turned her to face him. "Sara . . ." he began, but just then the door of the house burst open and a beautiful young woman, flame-red hair flying about her face, came running toward them.

"Dominic!" she exclaimed joyously, and Dominic dropped his hands from Sara's shoulders.

When the girl reached them, she stood on tiptoe and kissed him soundly on the lips.

Sara stepped back, shocked. Dominic had grasped the girl's waist, whether to pull her to him or push her away, Sara could not tell.

"Lydia!" he said, obviously surprised by her appearance.

Just as quickly as she had flung herself upon him, the girl pulled away and took a few steps back. "I'm sorry, Dominic. I was just so glad to see you!" Her large green eyes sparkled coquettishly and her smile was captivating.

Then she noticed Sara and the smile disappeared.

"Lydia, this is Sara, your Uncle Simon's wife, who . . ."

"Yes, yes," she interrupted him, the sparkle in her eyes turning to a cold scrutiny that made Sara cringe. "Mother told me about her. I hardly even remembered that I had an uncle. Aren't you awfully young to have been married to Uncle Simon?''

Her question caught Sara unaware, and she didn't know what to say.

"Sara, this is Lydia, Catherine's daughter," Dominic completed the introduction.

"I'm happy to meet you, Lydia," Sara said politely but without conviction, ignoring Lydia's question about her marriage to Simon. With her own eyes she had seen the familiarity between Lydia and Dominic. She could scarcely believe the boldness of the girl in kissing Dominic like that, in front of her. It certainly had not been a charming little kiss like the one Dominic had given her.

Sara suddenly felt very foolish, and very young. Dominic was a sophisticated man of the world, no doubt used to women throwing themselves at him. She, Sara, was a simple country girl, to whom a kiss meant far more than it obviously did to him.

Sara began to suspect that Dominic had been nice to her for Catherine's sake. He had entertained her for two mornings, but now that Lydia was here. . . .

"Please excuse me," Sara said, "I'm a little tired." She gathered her skirt in her hands, fully aware that Lydia had recognized the dress as her own, and climbed the remaining steps to the veranda. She glanced back only briefly before going into the house, but it was time enough to see Lydia throw her arms around Dominic's neck once more.

CHAPTER 4

AT LUNCH THAT DAY Sara learned more about Catherine's only child. Lydia had been visiting friends in Charleston for several weeks and gaily recounted her adventures to her mother, practically ignoring Sara's presence at the table.

She was a spirited person, short of build, and buxom, like Catherine. Her enthusiastic account of her escapades in Charleston was undaunted by Catherine's disapproval.

"Oh, Mama, you're so old-fashioned!" she pouted, tossing about her glorious mane of red hair. "Charleston is just teeming with devastatingly handsome men, and could I help it that every one of them tried to sweep me off my feet?" She laughed charmingly. "Of course, not a one could compare to Dominic. He is by far the most magnificent man I have ever met." Her green eyes softened to a dreamy glow.

"He *is* very nice," Sara commented.

Lydia eyed her with calculation. "To have taken you for a buggy ride, yes."

"And he showed me Charlottesville yesterday."

"Really?" Lydia's look turned scathing. "Mama, I understand that poor Sara has nothing suitable to wear, having come from that backward place in Pennsylvania, but did you have to loan her my favorite morning dress?" To Sara she said, "Didn't Dominic wonder why you were wearing my clothes?"

"He didn't mention it at all."

"Such a gentleman," Lydia cooed.

"You needn't worry any more about Sara's borrowing your clothes, Lydia," Catherine said firmly. "Tomorrow we'll be visiting the dressmaker."

"Catherine, you mustn't do that," Sara protested. She was touched by the woman's generosity, but she would be leaving soon. Buying new clothes was unnecessary.

"Nonsense. I want to. Now that Lydia is home, she'll be needing her own garments, of course, although I'm sure she won't mind sharing some accessories, will you dear?"

"Mother . . ."

The next day was one of the most exciting Sara had ever experienced. Catherine took her to several talented dressmakers in Charlottesville and Sara was introduced to a world of tape measures and pins and needles and feminine beauty which she had only imagined existed. There was a continuous parade of ready-made gowns in cotton and challis and wool, in all the popular colors of lavender, blue and pink checks, dove, fawn, and yellow. Then there were fine brocades and velvets that could be sewn especially for her, and cloaks, pelisses, nightgowns, silk stockings, hats in straw and felt and velvet, shoes, parasols, and jewelry, all awaiting her approval and Catherine's.

After looking at so many lovely things, Sara was exhausted—more from the guilt she felt in Catherine's expenditure than in physical fatigue. Why, she wondered, did Catherine insist on making so many purchases, when Sara would very likely soon be returning to Pennsylvania? There would certainly be no occasion to wear the extravagant gowns in her simple farm community.

After dinner that night, Sara and Catherine withdrew into the library to relax from the hectic day of shopping. Lydia, saying she had a headache from too vigorous a ride with Dominic that day, excused herself from their company and went to her room upstairs.

A servant had laid a fire in the stone fireplace and it crackled and hissed, spreading its warmth throughout the room. Steaming mugs of chocolate rested upon the hearth. Beside them, on a gold-rimmed china tray, nestled two small pastries with pink and white icing.

Sara looked around her, at the heavy velvet draperies, damask settees, and tapestried chairs in rich hues of yellow and lavender. The room was softly lit by oil lamps standing mutely on the several richly carved oak tables, and she felt a sudden deep contentment. Was it acceptable for her to feel that way—or was it very wrong? She felt pulled between two opposing lifestyles: one simple, even frugal; the other, glamorous, often extravagant and seemingly sinful when so many other people, many of whom she knew personally, had so little.

"You're troubled about something, aren't you, Sara?" Catherine questioned her gently.

A weary sigh escaped Sara's parted lips. "Am I slipping into sin because I like the new clothes you bought me, and appreciate the beauty of this lovely home, and the delicious and abundant food I am enjoying every day?"

Catherine gazed at her with affection. "No, Sara, I don't think it is wrong. Doesn't the Bible say that every good and perfect gift comes from above? As long as we don't covet what others have, work honestly for what we receive, and give credit to the

Lord as the source, wealth itself is not sin. There is not a day that passes that I do not thank Him for His goodness to me."

"And, dear Catherine, you so generously share your wealth with others less fortunate than yourself, I know, for you have shared so much with me."

Catherine smiled. "It is a strange paradox, Sara, that the more I give, the more I seem to receive."

Sara thought about that as she leaned back on the small loveseat beside the fire and took up her needlework. She wanted to accept Catherine's reasoning, but she couldn't quite. Not yet.

Her eyes drifted to the bookcases lining two of the four walls. She wondered which books among the hundreds displayed there were the ones Dominic had in mind for her. He had probably forgotten all about his promise to select them for her—now that Lydia had returned. No doubt the lovely girl was occupying all his thoughts.

"Catherine," she asked, "tell me about Dominic's family. Do they all live with him at The Willows?"

Catherine stared at Sara. "Why do you ask?"

Sara shrugged her shoulders. "I'm just curious. He has such a lot of land that I assumed someone must share his home."

"Did you ask Dominic?"

"Yes, and he reacted very strangely to my question. In fact, he didn't tell me anything at all. Is there some secret I should not know?"

"Not a secret, Sara. Just pain. Dominic never talks about his parents, who, unfortunately, are dead. I'd rather Dominic tell you what he wants you to know. His friends have learned never to mention the subject. You might be wise to do the same."

Sara felt a gentle rebuke behind the kindly advice, and her curiosity was aroused at what possible reason Dominic could have for not wanting to discuss his parents. If she had known anything about her own parents, she would have loved telling everyone about them.

She returned to her sewing, and Catherine picked up the book of poems she had begun reading several nights before.

This time of day was becoming special for Sara and Catherine, for they both enjoyed the quiet of the evening hours and the congenial company of the other. In the week since Sara's arrival at Grand Oak, they had spent every evening in the library together. Such shared moments were forging a deep bond of intimacy between the two.

Sara tried to concentrate on her sewing, her slim fingers guiding the narrow needle and thread through an intricate design on the muslin cloth, but her mind wandered to thoughts of Lydia. She sighed wistfully at the sad truth that mother and daughter shared few interests. They were often at odds with each other, and Sara was shocked at Lydia's sharp tongue and rudeness to her mother, and to the servants who shied away from her.

How different Catherine was—so gracious and kind, and forever considerate of others. No wonder Dominic was so fond of her. *Dominic*. Sara's heart skipped a beat as she thought of the handsome, enigmatic man who had become a part of her life. In truth, there were not many moments when she did not think of him. And it had all started with the kiss. . . .

"Are you feeling all right, my dear?" Catherine was asking her, and Sara looked up guiltily, wondering how long her sister-in-law had been addressing her while she was reliving that brief exciting moment with Dominic. "Did the day tire you?"

"The day was far too exciting to tire me, Catherine. I'm still thinking of all the beautiful things you purchased for me. You're very generous. How shall I ever repay you?"

"Repay me? What nonsense. When a woman is as

old as I, and has more than enough money, she has the right to buy whatever pretties she desires for someone she cares for a great deal.''

"But they were so expensive," Sara went on, laying down her sewing, the wonder of it still in her eyes. "Whenever will I wear them all? I cannot stay much longer with you. Then what will become of those lovely things? I could never take them back with me to the Society.''

Catherine frowned. "Please don't speak of leaving, Sara. You've only just arrived, and I'm enjoying your visit so very much. Frankly, I wish I could persuade you to stay with me forever. You're becoming more and more precious to me as the days go by. You've brought real happiness into my life, Sara. I thank you for that.''

Sara set aside her needlework, rose, and approached Catherine's chair. Then, kneeling in front of her, Sara clasped the other woman's hands in her small ones.

"It is I, Catherine, who must thank you for giving me so much. Oh, not just the gowns and bonnets—I mean your affection, your caring . . . I—I have come to realize more than ever how very much I have missed in not having a real family. . . .''

"Then stay with me," Catherine urged, leaning forward. "Make a new life for yourself here. Allow me to help you. I can give you whatever you need or want.''

Sara rose and went to stand in front of the fireplace. "You're so very kind, and the temptation to stay is strong, but I must not succumb to it.''

"Why not?''

"Because I belong with the Society, with the MacReadys. I have an obligation to them.''

"And what about the obligation to yourself, Sara dear? Don't you have the right to live a full life?''

"When Simon died, my life ended, too." However

49

resolute her words, Sara's voice was small and wistful.

Catherine left her chair and hurried to Sara's side, twisting her hands in agitation. "You're not telling me that you're going to be true to his memory forever—that you plan never to marry again?"

"Yes. That is my decision," Sara replied softly.

"But you mustn't do that, my dear! You're too young, too fine a person to retire from life! There is a man out there somewhere, who needs your love. There are children who should be born. You would be a marvelous mother. You cannot . . ."

"Please stop!" Sara whirled around to face Catherine. "Don't fill my head with dreams that can never be fulfilled," she pleaded.

Catherine grasped Sara's shoulders. "Why can't you have dreams? And why can't they be fulfilled?"

"Because she is a saint," interrupted the resonant voice of Dominic Lansford coming from the door where he stood jauntily posed, having overheard most of their conversation. "And saints are not really alive, are they, Sara? You would prefer to return to your precious Society and be counted among the living dead, honoring your departed husband by sacrificing your own life."

A cynical smile twisted his lips and he came across the room to stand in front of the two women. He was casually dressed in brown riding breeches and a deep tan shirt open at the neck, and Sara tried to still the excitement she felt at seeing him again.

"Dominic, you're being rude," Catherine chided him. "This is of the utmost importance, and Sara and I are trying to think through her situation."

He shook his head. "There is nothing to think through, Catherine. Sara has made up her mind to return to the Society. Isn't that true, Sara?"

The coldness in his eyes was like a slap in the face, administered by his own hand. Why was he two people—one who was warm and caring and fun to be with; another who only surfaced when they were talking about the Society—uncaring, then, and prejudiced and not at all kind?

Gone was the friendship he had offered her just the day before, when they had sat close to each other in the carriage and he had gently caressed her cheek and . . .

"Yes, that is true. I must leave soon," Sara said, a peculiar sadness wrenching at her as she spoke the fateful words.

"You see," Dominic said, looking directly at Catherine, "the girl has made up her mind. She prefers to live simply—and alone."

Catherine stared at Dominic, then at Sara. "Please. Let's be seated and discuss this calmly and rationally." It was an order, not a request.

Sara instantly felt remorse, for she saw the anguish in her sister-in-law's face. Obediently, she sat, then blushed scarlet when Dominic took a place beside her on the velvet settee.

"You're very kind to be so concerned for my future, Catherine," Sara began, "but Dominic is right. I cannot live here. I don't belong. I am a simple country girl."

"You need a husband to look after you," Catherine argued gently.

"I need no husband. I can be content by myself."

"No one is completely happy alone," Catherine sighed. "I know that only too well. Sara dear, stay here. Learn our way of life. It will enrich you, enable you to be all that you can be. You will find a suitable husband, and he will be the most fortunate of men to have such a sweet wife. Wouldn't that be so, Dominic?"

"Sometimes, Mother dear," Lydia's harsh voice broke in before Dominic could answer, "a man wants more than sweetness." She swept into the room.

"Too much of anything can make one ill, or worse still, disinterested. Besides," she tossed her head saucily and came to stand beside the settee where Dominic and Sara were sitting, "I think a man needs spice along with sugar."

She laid a possessive hand on Dominic's shoulder, but he rose and walked a few paces away.

"A real man," Lydia went on, "needs a real woman. I think Sara has made the right decision never to marry again."

"Lydia," Catherine cut in sharply, "your opinion was uncalled for."

"But, Catherine," Dominic spoke up, "if Sara has made up her mind, what else can be done about it?"

Sara looked up at Dominic and was surprised at the intensity in his gaze. Did he want her to go or to stay? she wondered in confusion.

In those seconds when he held her to him with the power of his dark eyes, Sara's mind darted back to the scene just a day before. Dominic had looked at her softly then. His hand had caressed her cheek even as his words had caressed her spirit: "Will you ever know the kind of love that could be yours . . . ?" he had asked. She could feel the touch of his lips on hers. A gentle stirring rippled through her.

"Sara," a voice far away was calling her name, but she was lost in a reverie from which she could not rouse herself. "Sara, are you all right?" It was Dominic speaking, and they were in Catherine's library, not sitting close together in Dominic's carriage.

"What's the matter with you?" Lydia's piercing voice rang through the room, with the same tone she used to address the servants whose duty it was to wait on her. It jolted Sara back to the present. "Are you speechless when a man addresses you?"

Sara looked from one to the other, then said as

calmly as was possible, "I'm very sorry. I'm afraid I was daydreaming."

"Oh?" Dominic said with surprise. "What could a proper young lady from your Society possibly be dreaming about?"

Lydia laughed. "You're right, Dominic. To dream means to have feelings, and I believe that nothing excites Sara. That religious community she was brought up in has taught her to subdue her feelings. Isn't that right, Sara?"

For just a moment, Sara thought she saw a spark of anger flash in Dominic's eyes, as though to say to Lydia that it was all right for him to mock her, but no one else. But the look vanished as quickly as it had appeared, and Sara was sure she had just imagined it.

"Both of you, stop it!" Catherine interfered. "I will not allow either of you to abuse Sara. Lydia, if you cannot be civil, then take yourself elsewhere."

"Mother . . ."

"Please don't quarrel over me," Sara pleaded, rising and placing her sewing in its tapestried bag. "There are things I must attend to in my room. So if you'll excuse me. . . ."

She started to walk away, but Catherine laid a restraining hand on her arm.

"No, Sara, I shall not excuse you. Dominic is here this evening at my express wish so that he may do us both a favor."

Lydia's brows arched curiously. "What can Dominic possibly do for Sara?" she asked petulantly.

Catherine stared at her daughter. "Dominic has come to teach Sara to dance."

"To dance?" Lydia gasped in disbelief. "Dominic is to teach Sara to dance? What on earth for?"

"Why, Lydia," Catherine chided her gently, "have you forgotten that it is only two weeks until the Winter Frolic?"

The look of puzzlement on Lydia's pretty face grew

53

even more pronounced. "No, Mother, of course I haven't forgotten Dominic's party. Why, it's the most important social event of the season. But what has that to do with Sara?"

Catherine smiled. "Dominic is planning, I am sure, to include Sara among his guests. Isn't that right, Dominic?"

"Of course," he answered gallantly after a pause. "It will be my honor to extend an invitation to the lovely Mrs. Parsons."

His eyes sought Sara's, but she avoided looking at him.

"You want Sara to attend Dominic's Frolic?" Lydia questioned in amazement.

"Yes, dear. Sara has not had the advantage of your education. I doubt that social dancing is practiced in the Society, and I don't want her to be embarrassed at the party when all the young men ask her to dance, and she doesn't know how. So, who better to teach her all the proper steps than the host himself?"

Lydia rushed to Catherine, her face contorted. "Have you forgotten, Mother, that Sara is a widow? I'm sure the young gentlemen will not be interested in her when there will be dozens of unattached girls there. She probably won't be asked to dance once. How utterly humiliating for her—and for us," she muttered under her breath.

Catherine scowled at her daughter's rudeness.

"Sara knows nothing of fancy balls and sophisticated society and proper conduct," Lydia continued her tirade.

"Lydia is right, Catherine," Sara agreed, upset at being the object of so much attention. "I don't belong at such a function."

"You really will enjoy it, Sara," her sister-in-law insisted. "And don't worry about your conduct. You have a natural charm that will win you many friends, and I shall personally teach you everything else you need to know. And Lydia," she turned to her distraught daughter, "I rather think Sara will be more popular than you foresee. Her innocence is refreshing, and she'll certainly be a delightful change from the silly and affected young women we know. Don't you agree, Dominic?"

Dominic smiled warily, recognizing his tenuous position between mother and daughter. "It might prove to be so, Catherine, and you know that I stand ready to assist you in any plan you may have."

He walked over to Sara who was not at all happy about what she was being forced to do, even though it had been planned by Catherine. Not only was dancing not practiced in the Society—it was forbidden. Sara had always adhered to the group's doctrines and traditions with a willing heart. She did not wish to change now.

She was startled from her thoughts when a strong hand took her right one and led her to the center of the room. "Shall we begin with the minuet, Mrs. Parsons?" Dominic's hand was warm, and her fingers trembled in his grasp.

"No, Dominic. Please don't."

"Every important ball begins with a minuet," he said evenly, ignoring her plea. "When you have mastered that, we shall move on to some of the favorite English folk dances, and then I'll show you a new dance I learned while visiting southern Germany on business. It is so new that not even the socialites in London have seen it, nor is it known here. But I'm going to introduce it at my Frolic, and you, Sara, shall learn it before any of the others."

"Dominic, you're very kind to help us in this way," Catherine thanked him.

"Mother," Lydia fumed, as she stared in open jealousy at Dominic holding Sara's hand, "this is outrageous! I cannot believe you would waste Dominic's valuable time. It will be a colossal failure."

Catherine's eyes narrowed angrily. "You must learn to trust my judgment, Lydia. Come along. We'll leave them alone. Instruction is always simpler without an audience."

Under protest, Lydia began to follow her mother out of the room.

"No, please wait," Sara pleaded. "I cannot do this, Catherine, even at the risk of offending you. Lydia is right again when she says that my learning to dance is a waste of Dominic's time and effort. I could never learn to do it well enough in just a few weeks to be seen at so grand a party." She lowered her eyes modestly, and when she lifted them, they were filled with distress. "Besides, I won't even be here then. I must return to the Society. I've been away too long already."

"You've been here barely a week," Catherine rejoined. "I shall be hurt if you leave now, Sara. It is the fondest wish of my heart that you stay long enough to attend Dominic's party with Lydia and me."

"But, Catherine . . ."

"Please don't disappoint me, Sara, my dear." She turned and left the room, pulling Lydia behind her.

Why didn't I tell Catherine that my conscience will bother me if I dance with Dominic? she pondered, disgusted with her slow-wittedness. But it was too late. She was alone with Dominic, and he was still holding her hand.

"Shall we begin?" It was a command, not a request, and Sara trembled at the prospect of what the rest of the evening held for her.

CHAPTER 5

"YOU'RE NERVOUS." Dominic said to Sara. "Your first lesson will be to learn how to relax."

"I have never danced before," she admitted, her eyes lowered.

Dominic grunted. "Forbidden by the Society, no doubt?"

"Yes."

Dominic turned Sara to face him and with his free hand tilted her chin so that she had to look up at him. "And do you think you will lose your soul if you dance with me now?"

"Please don't make fun of my upbringing. The Society has its reasons for feeling as it does about dancing, and I haven't suffered unduly because I've never done so."

Dominic smiled slightly and nodded his head. "I apologize if I have offended you, madame."

Sara turned away, pulling her fingers gently from Dominic's grasp. "I should have told Catherine how strong my convictions are against this."

"And she would have understood. However, I

think you'll find dancing very enjoyable, and although I'm no expert on spiritual matters, I feel fairly certain that you will not be committing a mortal sin if you move your feet across the floor and allow me to touch your hand every now and then."

Sara glanced up at him. Again, his eyes were mocking her and what she believed. Should she remain true to those teachings, or give in and do as Catherine wished? Sara did not want to offend this woman who had been so loving to her. She also knew she could never go to Dominic's party unless she were fully prepared to participate along with all the other guests.

No one at the Society would ever know, she reasoned, and surely God would forgive her this one temporary digression from her standards.

She faced Dominic. "For Catherine, who is the kindest of all women, I shall do it."

She looked at him directly and felt a little foolish when the corner of his mouth turned up in derision.

"I realize this is a momentous occasion," he said, "and I shall do my best to make it an enjoyable one for you. And please understand that I, too, am slave to Catherine's wishes. She is one of the most remarkable women I have ever known, and I would move heaven and earth to please her. Perhaps you and I together can show her just how much we appreciate her."

He took Sara's hand and positioned her so they stood side by side, arms extended to each other, fingers barely touching. Dominic extended his inside leg slightly ahead of the other and pointed the toe of his foot. Sara imitated him.

"We're ready to begin," Dominic stated. "Dancing, you know, is as old as man himself. In the beginning man danced, quite naturally, to express his feelings."

Dominic showed Sara a few steps and they repeated

them over several times until she was able to execute them with some degree of ease.

"Then he wanted to reach powers greater than himself—nature. So he emulated the swaying of the trees, the rushing of water, and the movement of the wind. Light, dark, heat, cold, all were shown respect through movements of dance."

Sara listened in awe to Dominic's words and found herself following his lead quite accurately.

"In time man's homage moved from the physical objects around him to the spirit that lay within him. Then his dancing took on the form of worship, a physical demonstration of his religious feelings. He danced in celebration of birth and adolescence, of marriage and death. He danced in joy, and he danced in sorrow. He danced when going into battle, and when returning from it."

Dominic glanced sideways at Sara. "I believe King David himself danced upon his return after a victory over the Philistines. Isn't that right?"

Sara couldn't help smiling a little as she acknowledged the statement with a nod.

"In time, the dance ritual became so elaborate that it took experts to properly express it, and the art of performing was born."

They stopped to rest and sat down.

"I never thought of dancing in the way you've described it," Sara said. "It hardly seems wicked, does it?"

"To be truthful, some of it is," Dominic said with a little laugh. "But I'll protect you from that form, Sara Parsons." He suddenly grew serious. "You're a woman a man wants to protect, to keep unsoiled and pure." He paused. "I'm sure your husband felt the same way about you."

His eyes drifted over her face. Long moments passed.

"We'd better continue," he said softly. He helped Sara to her feet and introduced to her the quadrille.

"This is usually done with three other couples, or sometimes seven," Dominic explained to Sara, who learned the five consecutive figures with no problem and earned a compliment from her teacher.

The lively *courante*, with its quick running steps was next, and it became increasingly difficult for Sara to keep up with Dominic's unmatchable stamina.

"Stop, please!" she begged, as he urged her faster and faster.

"You mustn't stop now!" he insisted. "You have to feel the vitality of this dance!"

He drove her on, though as he did so he began to laugh at Sara's expressions of exhaustion.

"Come, come," he urged her, "surely you can keep up with an old man. I'm at least ten years older than you."

"But you have the endurance of a bull," Sara gasped, feeling her hair slipping out of its pins; some of it falling about her face.

Without warning Dominic slipped his arms around her and she, laughing and without thinking, collapsed into them, in great relief.

"Please, please," she begged, "I have no more breath."

He stopped dancing and just held her. Sara rested her head against his chest, not even realizing what she was doing. Her breathing was labored and she closed her eyes and took deep breaths at Dominic's instruction. Gradually she relaxed and raised her head to look into Dominic's face, her eyes bright with the conquest of learning. He was tired, too, he admitted to her, and a light sheen of perspiration filmed his cheeks and temples.

Sara began to pull away from him, but Dominic's arms tightened around her. In his eyes she saw something that startled her. It was a look of desire, and not one she had seen often, for in the Society men did not gaze at women like that, at least not in public. In Simon's eyes she had seen it several times, but he had always reacted to the feelings that had caused it by hastily walking away, leaving her to think he was displeased with her.

Now, as Dominic's eyes darkened ominously, she wondered if he would leave as precipitously as before. But his look held a question this time. Drawing her still closer to him, he slowly lowered his head toward hers, his fingers lifting her face upward.

Sara knew he was going to kiss her, and did not even think of denying him. Quite naturally, as though she had done so a hundred times before, she allowed her lips to be kissed.

Dominic's mouth on her hers was sweet and gentle, tentative, as though he felt she might pull away from him. But Sara clung to his strong arms, giving her lips to him, enjoying the thrill that surged through her and made her feel so wonderfully alive.

She had never felt such ecstasy, prolonged when Dominic's lips traveled tenderly over her face and down the slender column of her throat. A new kind of emotion enveloped her—and she felt a sudden awareness of what it meant to be a woman.

Whenever she had seen couples together in the Society, they had always been circumspect, behaving with perfect propriety. She had never suspected they could have such explosive feelings for each other in private. She ran her fingers through the thick dark hair that covered Dominic's ears, and raised her lips to his.

Dominic accepted her kiss, then lifted his head and gazed deeply into her eyes.

"Sara, Sara," he murmured huskily, "what am I to do with you?"

"What do you want to do with me?" she whispered

in return, innocent of the provocative question she had asked.

She felt him stiffen. "Are you really so naïve, my dear?" he said sharply. "You have been a married woman."

He dropped his hands from her waist and stepped back, as though he had been struck. Here was the same displeasure with her that Simon had displayed, only Simon had never kissed her the way Dominic just had.

"Did I do something wrong?" she asked humbly.

Dominic shook his head. "You did nothing wrong, Sara. It is I who must apologize."

"Why?"

"For taking advantage of you."

"Did you?"

He stared at her quizzically, as though not quite believing her. "I think we have practiced enough for one night. You're tired, as am I. Otherwise, I would never have allowed what just happened. . . ."

"I've disappointed you in some way." Her eyes were sad pools of smoky blue that gazed up at Dominic, silently pleading for his forgiveness. Yet she could not guess what she had done to offend him.

He looked at her a long time before he spoke. "You did not disappoint me, Sara. In fact," his voice grew soft and he took her gently by the shoulders, "you please me very much."

"Is that why you kissed me?"

"Yes."

"Do you want to kiss me again?"

He dropped his hands in exasperation and turned away from her. "Good heavens, woman, yes! But I'm not going to." He faced her. "You're going upstairs to bed, and I'm going home—now."

"I could never regret kissing you, Dominic."

"Sara, you don't know what you're saying."

"But Dominic, no man has ever . . ."

He stared at her. The silence was profound.

"No man has ever what, Sara?"

Sara lowered her eyes, suddenly embarrassed.

"Surely you're not saying that you've never been kissed like that before?" he asked incredulously.

"Y—Yes." Long delicate lashes lay along her silky cheeks as she lowered her eyes modestly.

"You can't mean that, Sara! You were married to Simon Parsons for six months."

His disbelieving gaze raced over her, then settled on her huge rounded eyes of blue, filled with bewilderment. His mind reeled with the implication of what she had just hinted at. He grabbed her by the shoulders and pulled her close to him.

"Explain what you said to me, Sara."

It was an order, and Sara trembled at the way he held her and the way he was watching her. His eyes blazed with an anger that she did not understand and his mouth was drawn tight against his teeth.

"I s—simply meant that . . ."

Dominic shook her. "That what?"

"Simon was not an . . . affectionate man. He did not easily display his emotions, or give . . . give way to them."

Sara swallowed hard. She wanted to die from humiliation. That she should discuss such a thing. And with Dominic, of all people! She felt the crushing grip of his hands on her arms. It was beginning to hurt. She winced and he saw her expression and immediately released her.

"I'm sorry," he said. "I thought at first you might be saying . . ."

"Saying what?" She looked up at him with all the innocence of a child.

"Nothing. Nothing at all."

He touched her cheek and smiled. The awful time of suspense was over and Sara's heart bounded with joy. Dominic was no longer angry with her! All she had let slip out was that Simon had not kissed her the way Dominic had. Was that so bad? Did Dominic think less of her because she'd told him? She hoped not.

Dominic led her to one of the settees and they sat down.

"Did you know Simon very well before you married him, Sara?"

Sara thought for a moment. "I knew him, but not well. We really didn't have much contact except seeing one another occasionally as we worked, and on the Lord's Day at services. I knew his first wife, too. She was a very nice person. I was sad when she died, and I remember that Simon wouldn't talk to anyone for a long time after that. She died in childbirth, and the child died as well. It was a boy. Simon never spoke of his wife or son to anyone, not even to me after we were married. I asked him about them once, but he told me nothing and ordered me never to mention it again."

"Did you love Simon?"

Sara shrugged her shoulders. "Love wasn't discussed in the Society."

"So you agreed to marry someone you barely knew, someone you didn't love?"

Sara brushed away a few strands of hair which had strayed onto her cheeks, then folded her hands in her lap. They were cold. She vacillated between wanting to share her former life with Dominic and being afraid to because of the censure that inevitably arose in him when they talked of the Society. It was there now.

"Simon spoke to me several times, and told me about his farm on which he grew corn and apples. He needed help with the farming and someone to care for his house. He showed me the land and the house which had two rooms and was very clean."

"Are you telling me that you married him in order

to help him in the fields and to care for his already clean house?'' Dominic's voice was derisive.

"I guess that sounds ridiculous to you."

"More sad than ridiculous. Few people nowadays want a marriage of convenience and every man I know wants to find a wife whom he can deeply love, a wife who will love him deeply in return."

Sara stood up suddenly, feeling a great need to defend herself. "Simon was a good man," she said hotly, "a godly man, and a hard worker. I knew he would always provide me with a home and the honor of his name, and would be a devoted father to our children. What more was there to consider?"

The anger welled up inside her like a burgeoning flood. She had nothing to be sorry for. Simon had been a good husband.

Dominic stood up and took hold of her hands that were clenched into tiny fists. "I seem to have said the wrong thing." A conciliatory grin did much to lessen Sara's ire. She was amazed, now, at how upset she had gotten. She had never spoken to anyone in the Society in the sharp manner in which she had just addressed Dominic.

Why was he so able to incite her to strong feelings? She seemed to have less control of herself when she was with him. It was very unsettling.

"You don't think like any other woman I know," Dominic stated, continuing to warm her hands in his.

"That's because I'm not from your world. Just forget what I say, if it bothers you."

"I can't do that."

"Why not?"

"Because sometimes you say things I need to hear."

"I don't understand."

"I'm not sure I do either. Or want to." Dominic expelled a deep breath and dropped her hands.

"Anyway, I enjoyed teaching you this evening. I hope you enjoyed it, too."

Sara relaxed under his friendly gaze. "I did. Thank you."

"You're a promising student. You caught on quickly."

Her heart skipped a beat at his praise. "I don't want to embarrass you and Catherine at your party."

"You won't. Believe that. Catherine will give you some hints, and you and I shall practice many times before that, Sara. One night is not enough to ensure your remembering the intricate steps. I'll come again tomorrow and we'll review everything before I show you one or two new dances."

"All right."

After Dominic left, Sara walked thoughtfully up the stairs to her room. In her mind she replayed all that had happened that night, and in particular she thought about Dominic's tenderness. He had spoken harshly to her afterward, though. Why? She feared she should not have allowed him to take such liberties with her.

Were Virginia men allowed to kiss women like that whenever they were alone? Was it something rather meaningless, done for the enjoyment of the moment, and then forgotten by both parties?

She must learn the answer to those questions if she was to conduct herself properly in this society where rules seemed far less strict than those by which she had been raised. In her Society no unmarried man would ever attempt to kiss an unmarried woman unless they were quite sinful and did it in secret. Once, when she was sixteen, a boy had found her in the barn alone, milking the cows, and he had tried to kiss her. She had hit him in the back with the little stool she had been sitting on. He hadn't spoken to her for many months after that. Then there was Simon. . . .

Sara breathed deeply and sank wearily down on the

bed. She mustn't think of Simon. He was dead, and she was alive, and Dominic had awakened her to emotions she had not known existed.

In the last few fragile thoughts before sleep overtook her, she savored again the feel of Dominic's lips on hers, his powerful hands holding her slender body against his own.

CHAPTER 6

THE WINTER FROLIC held at The Willows was like no party Sara could have imagined in one of her most vivid dreams. Later she tried to record in her journal every last detail of what had happened to her on that day, but there was so very much to tell, and her pen flagged as she drifted off from time to time into this remembrance or that.

It had started early in the morning when Catherine had come floating into her room with an exquisite gown draped over her arm—the one Sara was to wear that evening.

"Time to get up," Catherine's cheery voice awoke her.

Back at the Society Sara had been accustomed to rising early, years of discipline having enabled her to jump out of bed before the first hint of morning's light. But since coming to stay with Catherine, she had been allowed to sleep later, and had gradually adopted the delightful habit of waking up leisurely, and staring out the window into space, lolling lazily in bed while listening to the first twitter of the birds outside her

68

window. If she chose to, she could eat her breakfast in bed instead of downstairs in the dining room. If she chose to, she could even go back to sleep.

More than once Sara had worried that she was becoming terribly spoiled, and that she would find it difficult to readjust to the rigid life of the Society.

She raised herself on one elbow and sleepily watched her benefactress carefully hanging the beautiful gown in the armoire, meticulously arranging the delicate folds of the velvet skirt. Then Catherine moved to the window, humming all the while, pushing aside the heavy draperies to let in more of the December sunlight.

"Brigitte is here, my dear," she said to Sara, "to make sure your dress fits perfectly. I hope you haven't gained any weight since you tried it on the other day. It's not easy to take out seams. But we shall see. Just a light breakfast for you today, Sara. Then we must begin on your hair. I have something unique in mind."

"My goodness," Sara laughed, "is it going to take all day to prepare me for this one gala event?"

"Of course, dear. It's all part of the fun. Dressing for such a party should not be hurried. One must allow time to imagine what it will be like, to indulge one's fantasies, to dream outrageous dreams. And I think you'll be surprised and pleased with the Winter Frolic. Dominic goes to great lengths to make this one of the two most important social events of the season."

"What is the other?" Sara asked, rubbing her eyes and yawning and wishing she could snuggle down into the covers for just a few more minutes.

"The Spring Ball, hosted by our beloved president, Thomas Jefferson. It is held at Monticello, and is every bit as exciting as Dominic's Winter Frolic, although just a little less glamorous."

Sara's eyes grew dreamy. "I would love to see that," she sighed.

Catherine pretended great interest in tidying a set of combs and brushes on a square mahogany table. "There is no reason why you shouldn't, my dear," she said lightly, and when there was no argument forthcoming from Sara, she smiled.

Sara yawned again and slowly slid out of bed, pulling her soft nightgown down around her long slender legs. "I'm very excited about tonight, Catherine, but also a little frightened. How will I ever remember everything you've taught me? What if I say the wrong thing, or laugh too loudly, or use the wrong utensil at dinner?"

"You have nothing to worry about. I assume you have worked as hard with Dominic."

"I've tried, and I honestly think he's pleased with my progress."

Sara's mind wandered back to the first night she had danced with him, remembering how much she had enjoyed the lesson, despite some serious doubts that she should be dancing at all. She also remembered, vividly, the greater thrill of the evening that had come when Dominic had taken her in his arms and kissed her, releasing in her a myriad of exquisite emotions.

Later, in her room, she had wondered whether such kissing and holding was a serious or playful thing between the men and women of Virginia, and whether Dominic thought less of her because of her willingness to do so. The question had been answered the very next night, when Dominic had come to give her another dancing lesson. He made no mention of what had happened between them the night before, nor did he attempt to kiss her again. Sara was not sure whether she was relieved or disappointed. A part of her wanted Dominic to sweep her off her feet and into the warmth and excitement of his arms, to capture her willing lips, to whisper her name into her hair as he had done just hours before.

But when he didn't do so, Sara knew that the affectionate embrace and kiss, that had set her heart wildly racing, had meant little to him.

The dancing lessons had continued for nearly two weeks, and Dominic had taught Sara so many steps that she was sure she would never remember them all. Also, she was worried that dancing with someone else would not be at all the same as dancing with Dominic. She voiced this fear to Catherine.

"You will move with the grace of an angel. Both ladies and gentlemen will whisper your name in admiration and wonder who you are."

"I hope no one asks me to dance."

"Oh, Sara, you may be sure a great many men will ask you."

Sara looked worried. "Will that be proper? My husband. . . ."

" . . . died well over a year ago. You are no longer in mourning. As a widow, even a very young one, you must be circumspect, of course, but if you act with your own unique dignity tonight, Virginia society will gladly welcome you. Especially the men."

Sara giggled. "Catherine, what a romantic you are. I am sure few men there will even notice."

Catherine smiled, a playful gleam dancing in her eyes. "They will notice you, Sara. I can guarantee that."

Sara, fully awake now, rushed over to Catherine and threw her arms around her. "You are the most wonderful woman I have ever known!" she exclaimed, her eyes sparkling like two crystal pools. "You have taken a total stranger into your home and treated me as a royal guest. You've been kind beyond belief, and caring of my feelings, and patient with my stupidity and backward ways."

"Hush, hush. No talk of that." Catherine returned

71

her hug, then stood back to look into Sara's angelic face. "It is the person you are, Sara, that makes it so easy to pamper and please you, and I am privileged to have been able to do so. I need someone to lavish my love upon."

"But there is Lydia. . . ."

Catherine shook her head sadly. "Lydia and I are not as close as I would like us to be. I'm not sure why. Perhaps it is because she's so independent, like many of the modern young women, and I am, unfortunately, more comfortable in a way of life in which women are quieter, more genteel, less demanding of men, more conscious of good manners and caring for the feelings of others. I know that Lydia is just trying to find her way in an often confusing world, but I find it impossible at times to understand her. It's hard to explain, nor should I try on this special day when all should be joy and gaiety." Her attempt to lighten the somber mood of her words did not escape Sara's notice.

She reached out and grasped both Sara's hands in hers, "But with you, Sara, it is different. It's as though you are my own daughter, rather than my sister-in-law. You and I have an uncommon rapport and understanding of each other that hardly needs to be spoken. You seem to be a younger version of myself." Catherine stopped and lowered her eyes. "I sound like a pompous old lady, don't I?"

"No, you don't," Sara denied. "I am honored and touched that you think we are alike. But I could never be the sophisticated, gracious lady you are, Catherine. I'm far too ignorant."

"What utter nonsense!" Catherine scoffed. "All you need is a little exposure to our ways. Then you will be the grandest lady of them all. But come, here is your breakfast." A servant girl, not much older than Sara, brought in a tray.

"Some fresh fruit and a few muffins with honey,"

Catherine inspected the tray and approved. "Just as I ordered. Thank you, Dora. After you have eaten, Sara, we must begin. The vision you'll become will take some time to bring about."

And so it began—the whirlwind of preparation to turn Sara into a princess, for that is how she felt. It was exciting but also frightening, as a bevy of people flitted about her that day, working with her dress, her hair, her skin, her nails, and even her toenails, although she could not imagine why her toes should need attention, confined as they would be within satin slippers.

Catherine explained. "You must feel beautiful from the top of your head to the tips of your toes."

And perhaps she was right, Sara concluded toward the end of the afternoon, for she felt more of a lady than she had ever felt before, and just before dusk fell over the rolling hills of Virginia, when she and Lydia and Catherine were on their way to the party in the large enclosed carriage reserved for special occasions, Sara felt as though she were truly of royal blood.

Just at that moment, unbidden, a sermon Elder Bates preached once on what it meant to be a child of the King rushed into her anxious thoughts. Yes, because she had given her heart to Christ, she was heir to the Kingdom of Heaven. All the extravagance she would be seeing tonight would be nothing compared to the treasures awaiting her in Eternity. She would have to remember that and not allow herself to be unduly impressed.

Nevertheless, she was eager to see Dominic's home—The Willows. The name, Dominic had told her, came from the presence of no less than eighty black willow trees scattered over the thousands of acres he owned, some of them rising to a height of sixty feet. More than two dozen of these trees bordered the wide and straight three-quarter-mile drive that led from the main road up to the house.

Now their large irregular branches stretched out naked over the road and the dormant winter grass, but in a few months those same branches would be laden with thin narrow leaves with tiny heart-shaped collars at their bases.

Sara longed to lean out the carriage window to catch a first glimpse of The Willows. Instead, she sat, ladylike, avoiding Lydia's studied look, her back stiff and not resting against the cushions of the handsome leather seat, her hands folded primly on her lap.

When the carriage stopped, she and Catherine and Lydia were helped out by well-dressed female slaves who straightened the skirts of their gowns, then hurried on to assist other arriving guests.

Sara tried to look discreetly straight ahead, but finally surrendered to an overwhelming curiosity to see all of what Catherine had told her was one of the most magnificent plantation houses in all Virginia.

Her mouth dropped slowly open, and her eyes widened as they swept from one end of the mansion to the other, and she promptly forgot her determination to remain unimpressed.

"Stop gaping, for heaven's sake," Lydia ordered sharply. "It's only a house. You're embarrassing us."

Sara didn't even hear her. She had fallen under the spell of the superb three-storied brick mansion painted white and gleaming like alabaster in the torchlight. A double row of six windows across the front revealed that many of the partygoers were already enjoying Dominic's hospitality within.

The house was located on a gently sloping knoll, surrounded by a beautiful lawn and park in which stood huge magnolias, tulip poplars, and enormous myrtles. According to Catherine, their great size was attributed to the unique stratum of marl which underlaid the rich land.

To one side of the house was the beginning of an enormous garden. "In the spring," Catherine said, "it

74

will be resplendent with roses, lilies, lilacs, English bay, and thousands upon thousands of daffodils."

Sara thought Dominic must have a great number of slaves just to care for the grounds, let alone the many rooms inside.

Down two pathways, leading left and right from the Great House, as it was called, and toward the rear of it, were a number of handsome outbuildings of white wood—dependencies—which Catherine said were the kitchen, laundry, icehouse, smokehouse, dairy, carriage house, and stables. The stables, in fact, comprised four or five buildings.

Because of the crowd of people, and because it was chilly, Catherine urged Sara up the eight wide gray stone pyramid steps that narrowed upward to the deep covered portico, flanked on either side by two large circular pillars.

Sara turned her head this way and that, trying to take in everything at once as they entered the magnificent marble doorway. Inside, the surroundings were even more breathtaking. Sara was awestruck.

Lydia sighed in disgust over her plebeian conduct and turned to greet friends with giggles and exclamations of delight. At first chance, she raced off with some of them without even asking Sara if she would like to come along. Sara caught the frown on Catherine's face as she watched her daughter disappear into a sea of billowing dresses.

The interior of The Willows was something a person could not take in all at once, so much was there to see. The great hall was wide and long and ended in the right rear corner in a magnificent circular staircase that swept upward, to the left, to the second and third floors and was wide enough to accommodate ten men abreast.

"Dominic hired a master woodworker from England to carve the wood throughout the house,"

Catherine told a wide-eyed Sara. "This hallway and staircase alone took over three years to complete."

"Look at the chandelier!" Sara exclaimed, raising her hand to point until she caught herself just in time. "It hangs all the way from the third floor to light this hallway."

As if in a dream, Sara floated over the delicate Oriental carpet on the floor which stretched to within a foot of the walls.

In her private assessment, Sara was neither aware of the bustle and chatter of the other guests around her nor of the interested scrutiny of several young men who stood at the end of the hallway, whispering among themselves.

Her eyes, never having been exposed to fine art, devoured the towering Renaissance tapestry in its ornate gold-edged frame that hung on the west wall near the front door.

"Are we allowed to sit here?" she asked Catherine as they passed between two scarlet sofas facing each other across the room. Catherine nodded her assent.

"This is Chelsea porcelain," Catherine advised, gesturing toward a long mahogany table on which the delicate vase and two deliciously scented bayberry candles had been placed. The candles were the only Christmas decoration in the entire hall.

Still bemused, Sara found herself being led through a graceful arched doorway and into the drawing room in which the dancing was to take place, and where the guests were generally gathered.

It was a mammoth room with oversized windows and mirrors and doorways, all lavishly decorated for Christmas with fresh evergreen boughs, their unique woodsy scent adding their own pungent pleasure to the occasion.

The magnificent furniture—George I high-backed walnut side chairs, chaise lounges and settees covered with superb silk damask, and tables with ball-and-claw feet—was pushed back against the walls. In a large fireplace in the center of the long west wall, a huge pine log was burning brightly. Two Dutch brass chandeliers shed benevolent candlelight down upon the excited guests.

"Sara," Catherine was saying to her, "I would like you to meet Alexander Marshall and James Randolph."

Sara slowly drew her eyes away from the glittering candles of the chandeliers and looked into the faces of two young men who were watching her with eager fascination. They did not seem much older than she, but having been born and reared in the wealthy society of Virginia, their manners were impeccable in approaching a young woman.

"Mrs. Parsons," James Randolph greeted her while reaching for and delicately kissing her hand, "welcome to Virginia. Allow me to say how very fortunate we are to have someone of your beauty to grace our state. I hope your visit will be a lengthy one."

"Thank you, Mr. Randolph," Sara replied. His wide blue eyes and large overpowering nose drew Sara's eyes to his face, although she had noted how elegantly he was dressed in buff-colored knee breeches of smooth velvet.

His friend, Mr. Marshall, was no less elegantly attired in a brightly colored waistcoat of green brocade. Not one, but two heavy watch fobs hung at either side, across the front of his sparkling white shirt. He, too, kissed Sara's hand, and looked at her so adoringly that she was embarrassed and glanced at Catherine in a silent plea.

Catherine took her arm. "I'm sure Sara will want to speak to both of you at greater length, and perhaps even to share a dance, but now I must take her away. There are many people waiting to meet her."

"Of course. We understand," James Randolph

said, bowing, and his nose twitched a little in his excitement, almost causing Sara to laugh.

Catherine whisked her away from the two young men and introduced her to so many people that the names became a jumble in Sara's mind and she knew she would never be able to remember all of them. A number of young unmarried men paid her extravagant compliments, and were so concerned that she have a memorable time that night, that Sara was quite touched by their sincere kindness.

"Jane Robertson," Catherine caught the attention of a young plumpish girl who looked to be about Sara's age, "have you been losing weight?"

The pretty girl with dark brown hair and crinkles at the corners of her sparkling eyes smiled broadly, showing slightly crooked teeth.

"I'm never sure whether I'm gaining or losing. The only way I can tell is how my clothes fit, and to tell the truth, Mrs. Throne, just today I had to let out the seams in this dress."

Catherine stifled a smile and leaned over to pat the girl's arm affectionately. "It doesn't show, my dear. You look truly lovely."

Jane Robertson's eyes glistened with gratitude. "Thank you, ma'am," she sighed, "though, gain or lose, I'll never be able to compete with Lydia or . . . or . . ." and she looked at Sara with such admiration that Sara was immensely flattered.

"Oh, Jane, I'd like you to meet someone very special to me—my sister-in-law, Sara Parsons. Sara knows only Lydia here tonight, but my errant daughter has flitted away to be with her friends. Would you be kind enough, Jane dear, to take Sara under your wing and be her special friend this evening?"

"Of course. A party is ever so much more fun when it can be shared." And Sara could tell from the happy sparkle in Jane's eyes that she meant it, and that they

78

would probably end up being good friends by the time the evening was over.

Catherine excused herself to greet other guests, and Jane clasped her hands tightly in front of her and looked directly into Sara's eyes.

"So, you are married to Catherine's brother?"

"I was. He died some time ago."

Jane drew in her breath. "I'm so very sorry."

The two girls stood looking at each other in awkward silence until Jane exclaimed, "Isn't this just far more than you had imagined it would be?"

Her eyes flashed with delight over the crowd of people who milled about, moving in and out of the drawing room-become-ballroom. "And have you ever seen such food?"

Sara had not, for the bountiful buffet table was in yet another large room. "There's even going to be a dinner served later. My mother will have to cut me out of this dress.

"There are so many people," Jane gushed on, her chubby cheeks flushed with excitement. "Why, absolutely *everybody* is here. You'd think since this is my second Winter Frolic, I'd be quite blasé about it all. But I just can't be, especially when our host is Dominic Lansford."

She gripped Sara's arm, and her mouth twitched in a funny way. "Have you ever met him?" Her eyes rolled and she hurried on without waiting for an answer from Sara. "Oh, he is the handsomest, most dashing man I've ever seen, and I just know I shall swoon when he enters the room. And should he ever look at me, well . . ." she fanned herself vigorously with a lovely lacquered fan with ivory handles, "I should never survive it."

Sara smiled, amused at the girl's open adoration of Dominic, agreeing silently with her that their host was indeed the most handsome, dashing man she had ever met. And since tonight, she had quite a few to compare him to.

"So, this is your second Frolic," Sara observed. "For me, it's the first."

"There is nothing like it!" Jane exclaimed. "Everything is so . . . so grand. It takes your breath away. The musicians will play all night, and there will be dancing. . . ."

"Yes, I thought there would be." Sara frowned, dreading the moment when she would have to prove the results of her host's instruction.

"But not until Dominic introduces it." Jane confirmed breathlessly.

"What do you mean?"

Jane sighed. "It's the most romantic thing you could imagine, Sara. Just before the dancing begins, Dominic will select one young lady from among his guests to be his very special partner. They'll dance, by themselves, in the center of this very room with everyone looking on. When they're finished, the rest of the guests may join them. Every girl here tonight prays she will be the lucky one. Oh, I would simply die if he chose me!"

"It's considered quite an honor, then?"

"Oh, my, yes! It's Dominic's way of saying he's interested in a particular girl, and every year for months after the ball, he is seen squiring her around town."

"Why hasn't he ever married one of them?" Sara mused aloud.

"Everyone wonders that. Dominic Lansford captures women's hearts left and right, but no one has yet captured his. It's quite the matter of gossip to speculate just what kind of woman he likes, and what kind he will eventually marry."

Sara frowned, puzzled. "But wouldn't he marry someone he likes?"

Jane looked aghast and leaned closer to Sara, taking

on a very grown-up air. "Don't you know, Sara, that men sometimes like a certain kind of woman for one thing, but quite another for marrying?"

"I didn't know that. Why should there be a difference?"

Jane stared at her. "Are you pretending with me?"

"No, Jane. I really don't understand what you're talking about."

"Well," Jane began in a breathless tone which betrayed her eagerness to share an adult, womanly piece of information, "men are very interested in . . . in physical pleasures."

Jane glanced at Sara to be sure she had her full attention, which she did.

"Some women enjoy that kind of thing, too, but others, like us, do not."

Sara stopped and turned curiously to Jane. "Why don't we enjoy it, too?"

"Because we're ladies," Jane whispered in a shocked little voice, "and must conduct ourselves with dignity and never ever let a man know that we welcome his lovemaking."

"Why is that?"

"Because . . . because," Jane stammered, "a proper lady simply . . . does not, unless she is married of course."

"Then it's all right?"

"I guess so, although I don't know for sure. All I know is that my mama is always telling me that no man marries a woman who is too loose with her affections."

Sara gulped. "I see. Then it is not the custom here in Virginia for an unmarried woman to allow a man to hold her and kiss her?"

Jane gaped at Sara. "Good heavens, no! If she does, and word gets around, she would be ruined. The subject of a scandal. A spotless reputation, Sara, is a girl's most valuable asset. Without it, she might just as well forget marrying any decent, well-bred gentleman."

"I see."

A sick feeling raced through Sara and left her knees weak and trembling. Not that she was interested in finding a husband. She definitely was not. But she hated the thought that, to Dominic, she was one of those bad women who enjoyed physical pleasures. Sara just prayed he had not told Catherine about her despicable behavior.

She sighed deeply, humiliated by her new knowledge and dreading the next time she would see Dominic, now that she knew he no longer respected her.

She and Jane stopped at a long table, laden with delicious-looking breads and pastries and cooked shrimp and a dozen other tempting morsels to be eaten easily with one's fingers. They enjoyed a few goodies; then Jane leaned close to Sara and confided, "Frankly, I think the whole thing is silly."

She picked up an oyster and dipped it in a creamy sauce, then popped the whole thing in her mouth. She ate with relish, though it made her cheeks puff out.

"What thing?"

"This game between men and women," she said, with her mouth still full. "Why shouldn't women be allowed to have fun, just like men?"

"'Fun'?"

"Yes. Why should it be perfectly all right for a man—like Dominic Lansford—to dally with as many women as he wants and earn for himself an enviable reputation among the men? Yet if a girl wants to do the same thing, no decent man will have anything to do with her."

"It doesn't seem fair, does it?" Sara hoped that was the right thing to say.

"No, it doesn't. It makes me sick! All the men care about is finding a woman no other man has touched!"

Sara didn't know whether to share Jane's anger, or to sympathize with her. How fortunate she was to have met Jane tonight. How much happier she would now be had she met her new friend earlier. But it was too late. The damage was already done.

She and Jane continued their walk. The aroma of the ballroom was a heady mixture of perfumes and colognes, and the earthy scent of pine boughs and burning candles. The two matching chandeliers each had at least three hundred candles, Jane told Sara, and their brilliant light was supplemented by more candles in exquisite gold wall sconces.

Groups of people milled about—in front of the fireplace, in private corners, or by the orchestra, which played soft music as a background to the constant chatter which went on among the happy guests.

"Look!" Jane grabbed Sara's arm, almost spilling the fruit shrub she was carrying in a small crystal glass. Jane was too well-mannered to point, but she nodded her head across the room. "There he is! Dominic Lansford!"

The mention of his name caused Sara's heart to pound. She looked in the direction Jane indicated.

There he was indeed, meandering through the crowd, greeting each guest, a generous smile on his handsome face. People flocked around him. Eager parents introduced him to their daughters. To each, Dominic inclined his head in a courtly acknowledgment of their acquaintance.

His superbly tailored garments hugged his muscular body—a dark blue coat cut across the waist but long in back; tight-fitting black trousers that buttoned at the ankle; a gleaming white waistcoat; a wide carefully tied white stock that contrasted sharply with the blackness of his thick dark hair.

Jane was on tiptoe, trying to get a peek at her hero above the heads of the sea of people in the room.

"Oh," she sighed, "didn't I tell you how very marvelous he is? Just one look from him turns my limbs to jelly. I would give just about *anything* to have him speak to me."

Sara watched Dominic nervously, fearful of meeting him again now that she understood certain . . . things, yet fascinated by his charm and good looks, wanting to be near him, just as did every other girl in the room. The wicked side of her—she knew now that she had a wicked side—resurrected the terrible secret that only she and Dominic shared. He had held her. He had kissed her.

What would Jane think if she told her that right now? She would no doubt be horrified at the loose conduct of her new friend, perhaps would want to have nothing more to do with her.

Suddenly, from across the room, Dominic's eyes found hers. He was, at that moment, lifting a young woman's hand to his lips, but he stopped in midair.

For that electric breath of time there was no one else in the room—just the two of them—Sara, bonded to Dominic in a gaze that captured her so completely she could not look away. And that moment of helplessness left Sara weak.

CHAPTER 7

SARA FORCED HERSELF to lower her eyes and started to move away, but Jane grabbed her and clung to her.

"He's coming this way!" Jane exclaimed, in a dither: "Oh, do you think we'll get to meet him? Where are my parents? How will he know who I am if they're not here to introduce me?"

Sara tried desperately to loosen Jane's hold on her so she could escape from Dominic, but it was too late.

"Mrs. Parsons," she heard his rich deep voice address her, "how nice to see you again." He did not kiss her hand.

Without even looking, Sara could feel Jane's surprise that Dominic Lansford should know her name.

Sara turned to face Dominic. His eyes leisurely examined her face and gown. Sara flushed with embarrassment, wishing she had worn a dress with buttons to her neck instead of the revealing black creation Catherine had insisted upon.

"May I say you look very beautiful tonight," he said smoothly. "Your dress becomes you." And then he was addressing Jane. "Miss Robertson," Dominic spoke her name with velvet tones, "how very kind of you to grace my party. I remember you from last year and wondered if you could come again."

Jane, for once, was speechless, unable to believe that Dominic knew who she was. An exquisite glow of ecstasy suffused her face.

"I know your father well," Dominic went on, ignoring the effect he was having on her. "We've had some business dealings in the past and lately he has shown some interest in buying one of my prize stallions. He's a fine man."

"Th . . . Thank you," Jane managed to stammer, her eyes glistening with tears of joy.

Dominic smiled, and with a slight bow he said, "I do hope, Miss Robertson, that you will save me a dance later on. I should be honored if you would."

"Of course."

Dominic bowed to Sara. "Mrs. Parsons." He moved on.

Sara looked after him for a moment, her emotions a hopeless tangle of anxiety and admiration.

Jane was in a state of personal shock, completely ignoring the fact that Dominic obviously knew Sara. "He wants to dance with me. I can't believe it. He wants to dance with *me!*"

"You're very lucky," Sara said, meaning it.

Jane turned and stared at her. "Did he ask you to dance with him, too, Sara?"

A lump formed in Sara's throat. "No, Jane, he didn't." Tears welled in her eyes. Even though Dominic had taught her the steps, he obviously didn't want to dance with her in front of his friends. Or maybe it was because there were so many other young ladies to choose from. Sara felt very . . . used . . . degraded by her own careless action with Dominic. Maybe that was why he didn't want to be associated with her.

She looked around her at the young beauties and

the handsome men who would someday become their husbands. Theirs would be a world of love, of home and children. Sara had had only a brief glimpse of that world the few times she had been with Dominic.

The Society had taught her early in life that there were "our sort of people," and "the other sort." She had been surrounded by her sort of people all her life—separated from "the other sort," except on those rare occasions when her adoptive parents or Simon had taken her to a town to buy supplies. But her sheltered existence had been shattered the day she had accompanied Catherine back to Virginia.

Now here she stood tonight, dressed in a gown far too immodest to her thinking, a participant in a way of life she could never hope to understand or accept.

The room was suddenly oppressively warm. She could hardly breathe. She thought she might even be sick. The many thoughts whirling through her head made the room spin around her. She needed air. She needed to stop thinking of the Society—of Simon—of Dominic.

She turned to flee but was accosted by Lydia and several of her glamorous friends.

"There you are," Lydia said accusingly, as though Sara had been hiding from her. "I want to talk with you. Girls, this is the Sara Parsons I was telling you about, my Uncle Simon's wife. She was married to him in Pennsylvania and they lived in some, uh, religious society. Isn't that right?"

"Yes," Sara answered, her head reeling in an attempt to forget her earlier troublesome thoughts, and fighting now to concentrate on what Lydia was saying to her.

"This is Jane Robertson," she managed to introduce her new friend.

"Oh, yes, I know Jane," Lydia dismissed the introduction disdainfully. "I saw you talking with Dominic Lansford. What did he want with you?"

The question was a rude one, and frankly, Sara thought, none of Lydia's business. But Jane was thrilled to be able to answer, "Mr. Lansford asked me to dance with him later!"

"Oh, is that all?" Lydia laughed, as did her three friends. "He says that to all the girls, Jane. It means nothing. I wouldn't count on his remembering you when the dancing begins. Dominic Lansford is a rover, and whatever pretty girl his eyes fall upon is in his favor for the moment—only for the moment. Then she's quickly forgotten, as they all are."

"Except you, Lydia," said one of her friends, a kind of wonder wrapping her words.

"Dominic and I *are* good friends," Lydia admitted, toying with a curl at the side of her elaborate hairdo. She smiled conspiratorially. "*Very* good friends."

Lydia's entourage giggled in supposed understanding, and Jane looked chagrined, her dream of dancing with Dominic cruelly shattered.

Sara resented Lydia's wanton disregard of her new friend's feelings, and even though it would be awkward for her to do so, she determined to find Dominic later and beg him to remember his promise to Jane.

"Shall we find your parents?" Sara said to Jane, wanting to get away from Lydia, and still feeling the need for some fresh air.

"Oh, don't go, Auntie Sara," Lydia purred. "I want you to tell the girls about the Society. They cannot imagine living in only two rooms, with no carpets on the floor. And, since you're the only girl our age who has been married, I told them you'd explain some, uh, some *things* about married life. You will, won't you, Sara?"

Sara stared at Lydia. "I don't know what you mean."

"Of course, you do! Did you enjoy. . . ah . . . the physical part of being married to my uncle?"

Sara's mouth flew open in amazement that Lydia

would broach such a delicate subject, and in public, no less. The very idea! Sara couldn't discuss something like that with Lydia and her friends, as though they were discussing the weather.

"I won't answer your question, Lydia," Sara said with as much finality as she could muster. "That's not the kind of thing a lady discusses casually."

"Don't be silly." Lydia's eyes burned with indignation. "Women talk of such things all the time."

"I don't."

"Why not? Or is there nothing to say?" Lydia stood with her hands on her hips, her mouth pursed in that defiant mannerism she had when she wasn't getting her way.

"Stop it, please, Lydia," Sara begged, appalled at her crudeness.

Lydia was distracted when the music began to crescendo, and she focused her attention on the end of the room where Dominic was standing.

"Victoria, do I look all right?" she asked one of her friends eagerly. "Martha? Susan?"

"Breathtaking!" they agreed in unison.

"He's sure to pick you," Victoria mouthed.

"How could he resist you in that Paris gown?" Martha added for good measure.

Sara knew that the Parisian gown had been purchased in Charleston and that Lydia was wearing it now against her mother's express wishes. But Lydia had haughtily denounced her mother's opinion as being 'hopelessly behind the times.' She had worn the dress anyway, certain that it would be one-of-a-kind at Dominic's famous party.

The gown was Grecian in style, a long diaphanous flow of white fabric, slit up the sides just above the knee, to reveal shapely limbs in flesh-colored tights. Sara thought the low-cut bodice scandalous, and Lydia received many a disapproving glare from the older women present. But from the men, both young and old, there were admiring glances.

"You'd better have told me the truth," Lydia warned her friends, knowing exactly how enticing she looked. "I want to be more beautiful than Dominic has ever seen me, when he chooses me to be his partner."

Sara began edging away, knowing this would be a good time to escape from the ballroom. She must find a place where she could be alone with her thoughts. Watching Dominic select Lydia as his partner would be the ultimate pain.

The music stopped and a hush fell over the room as Dominic began his walk. All eyes were focused on the tall, well-built man with the captivating dark eyes. Who would the lucky young lady be? Whoever she was, the woman of Dominic's choice would be the most talked-about girl in Albemarle County.

Dominic meandered slowly through the crowded room giving each beautiful young woman a look of careful scrutiny before he passed by.

Lydia was still preening as Dominic made his way toward her. Sara had succeeded in inching her way to the back of the crowd away from Lydia. She was, though, irresistibly curious about whom Dominic would choose, while shamelessly hoping it would *not* be Lydia.

But Dominic was pausing in front of Lydia!

The girl smiled and lifted her head proudly as her three friends twittered audibly. Jane stood transfixed in the presence of her hero, while Sara shrank even further back.

But Dominic stepped past Lydia, past her three friends, past Jane. Gentlemen inclined their heads in acknowledgment and ladies swept their bouffant skirts aside to allow him room to pass.

When he came to Sara, he extended his hand to her, fastening his mesmerizing gaze on her. There was not a sound in the room. Only the pounding of Sara's heart that, she felt, surely could be heard by all.

"Mrs. Parsons, would you do me the honor of dancing with me?" Before she could say no, before she could run away, Sara felt Dominic's fingers grasping her hand and gently pulling her away from the crowd.

No, wait! she wanted to cry out, but the words would not leave her dry throat. *You can't want to dance with me*, she thought in turmoil. *I barely know the steps, and all these young women have known them for years. And they're so beautiful, and I'm not at all beautiful, and I know that secretly you despise me for being too willing to let you hold me and kiss me. . . .*

Dominic, of course, did not hear her silent terrified cry for help, nor did he release her. Instead, he held her hand firmly and led her to the center of the room. The guests applauded his choice.

Dominic gazed at Sara, and her knees grew weak. She could not fathom why he had chosen her.

The room was getting darker, for the servants were snuffing out the candles along the wall. Soon, the people hovering at the sides of the room were lost in shadow and only the lights from the chandeliers above were shining down on them, like a magnificent spotlight, glorifying the actions of the man and the woman who stood alone beneath them.

"Don't be nervous," Dominic whispered to her. "You are the most beautiful woman here."

Sara knew that wasn't true, but she did feel very special as Dominic's dark eyes swept over her from head to toe, taking in the lacy pleated ruff in pale pink that framed her creamy throat, the exquisite velvet gown that fell from a high waistline to the floor without pleat or gather, the charming tendrils about her face that had escaped their confining satin ribbon, the thick luxuriant hair that tumbled down her back in silvery waves.

For the first time in her life, through Dominic's admiring eyes, Sara felt truly feminine, truly beautiful. A sweet self-confidence lifted her head, straightened her shoulders, imbued her with something she had never had before—an awareness of herself as someone unique.

The transformation was not entirely due to the beautiful clothes she was wearing, Sara well knew. It had come gradually, under Catherine's tutelage and example, and Dominic's as well. Tonight Sara liked the woman she was becoming.

"You are the most beautiful creature in the world, Sara," Dominic whispered once more. Sara met his gaze unashamedly, as strange and wonderful sensations coursed through her.

Dominic positioned himself to begin the dance, and Sara did the same, as she had been taught, but her heart was pounding and her fingers tingled where Dominic touched them.

CHAPTER 8

THE MUSIC PLAYED, and the spectators watched, bedazzled, as the handsome couple made their way through the intricate steps of the dance. Sara was suddenly conscious of having so many eyes peering at her every move. She grew stiff and unresponsive, and even though Dominic urged her several times to relax, she found herself unable to do so. She wanted only to finish and be allowed to evaporate into anonymity.

When it ended, the guests applauded in anticipation of being asked to join their host. But that did not happen. Instead, Dominic signaled the musicians to begin another tune. This one was hauntingly beautiful and slower, with a rhythm different from the first.

Dominic turned to Sara. "Do you remember the waltz I taught you?" Only she could hear his soft-spoken words. "No one in this room has ever seen one. Sara, would you honor me further by dancing it with me?"

Dominic did not wait for her answer, but turned to face her. As the poignant chords filled the room, he stepped closer and slowly, deliberately, placed his right hand on Sara's waist.

A murmur of surprise rippled through the crowd as he took Sara's hand in his.

"Don't mind the oohs and ahs," he told her. "They have never seen a dance where a man holds a woman in his arms as I am about to hold you."

He pulled her closer, and even though she was still at arm's length, there was, indeed, a reaction from the curious spectators.

"Who is she?" they asked each other. "Where does she come from?"

The music flowed enchantingly in three-quarter time, and Dominic and Sara glided across the floor, becoming a part of the graceful melody that drifted into every corner of the ballroom. There was a romantic aura to the waltz, as Dominic and Sara whirled about, her eyes lifted to his, his eyes seeing no one but her.

"Thank you for sharing this moment with me," he murmured as she began, at last, to relax.

"It is I who am honored."

His eyes traveled over her flushed face, drinking in her rare beauty, while the spectators became more and more curious, and Lydia burned with an intense jealousy she vowed to repay.

"Happy?" he asked.

"Mmm, yes," Sara answered dreamily. She felt herself becoming pleasurably pliant in Dominic's arms.

His arm tightened at her waist and Sara felt herself slipping into another world where only she and Dominic existed. The touch of his hand, the strength of his arm around her, his eyes looking so deeply into hers, filled her with a sweet euphoria unexcelled in her experience.

"I could go on like this forever," she said, her eyes closed, her head tilted to one side.

"With me?"

She opened her eyes and smiled. "Of course. No one else knows how to waltz."

Dominic threw back his head and laughed. "A cruel blow!"

"It wasn't intended to be," Sara laughed in return.

He looked at her for a long time before he spoke, and then there was a strange huskiness to his voice. "You are so beautiful when you laugh, Sara, and you don't do it nearly enough, you know."

"Are you requesting that I laugh more often?"

"Indeed. Particularly in my presence."

"If that is your command, sir, then I must humbly obey."

He smiled. "Are you really so docile that I simply have to ask and you will do whatever I bid you to?"

Sara fell prey to his bantering tone. "Ask what you will," she teased, "I'm yours to command."

He slowed their steps. "Then stay, Sara. Become a part of my world. Learn to live, and be happy."

"I know how to live—I have done so for nearly twenty years. And," she added firmly, "the Society makes me quite happy."

"You don't know what happiness is."

"And you do?"

He paused, ignoring her question. "Catherine loves you like a daughter. Hasn't she treated you so?"

"Yes, yes, she has, and I love her for it, too. But I can't. . . ."

"But of course you can," Dominic interrupted sharply. "The choice is yours. Leaving the Society is up to you. And Catherine will help you. Then when you marry again—"

"No!" Sara cried, stepping back from him, almost ending the dance. "I will never marry again. What must I do or say to convince you that I'm serious and will not be persuaded otherwise?"

"Your husband is dead. Nothing else ties you to the Society."

"Except a lifetime of love and concern and a way of life I respect and want to be a part of."

Dominic scowled. "You are dead, too, little Sara. You just don't know it."

Immediately his eyes softened with regret. He drew her closer and an earnestness was evident in his strong face.

"Your laughter tonight, Sara, was the sweetest music I've heard in a long while. Your smile lit up my home more than a thousand candles on a hundred candlesticks. Did you know, Sara, that when I first met you, you neither smiled nor laughed? Why do you suppose that was?"

"I don't know."

"But I *do*. You seem to believe Simon's death has destined you for a life alone, your only occupation that of servitude in someone else's home."

"Do I?" Sara pulled away from him abruptly, forcing Dominic to drop his hands. "And *you* are an overbearing man who seems to believe only his way of life is best—for everyone. Well, not for me!"

Dominic looked aside and noticed puzzled expressions on the faces of his guests as they witnessed his quarrel with Sara. The music continued but their waltzing ended.

"Meet me in an hour in the library," he ordered Sara under his breath.

"I won't. . . ." She started to walk away.

He grabbed her arm fiercely and pulled her back to him. His eyes burned into hers. He was not used to being refused, and she knew it.

"This is not a request, Sara," he rumbled ominously. "I will expect you within the hour."

Walking a few paces away he curtly signaled that the general dancing could now begin, but the guests only tentatively moved onto the floor to start a minuet, their interest lying more with the sudden disagreement between their host and his lady of mystery.

Sara's face burned with humiliation. Curious eyes stared at her, all of them having seen Dominic flare in anger.

Somewhere across the room, Lydia stood in smug amusement. Lowering her head, Sara ran off the dance floor and lost herself in the crowd of people milling at the sides of the room. She had to get outside. She was suffocating.

She pushed her way through a heavy door and was shocked at the biting cold of the air which met her uncovered flesh. A few deep breaths helped, but the pain of her experience with Dominic was too fresh.

"What do you call the dance you have just executed so exquisitely?" A man's voice addressed her from nearby.

Sara whirled around, unable to see anyone in the darkness of the night that engulfed the veranda. A man emerged from the shadows to her left. Sara backed away, startled.

"Please forgive me," he said. "I didn't mean to frighten you."

He was young, though older than Sara. Not much taller than she, his enormous gray eyes shone with kindness and interest.

Sara shivered as a sharp wind whipped at her bare arms.

"Here, put this on. It's cold tonight."

The stranger whisked off his double-breasted coat and gently placed it around Sara's shoulders. She murmured her thanks and looked closer at the kind stranger.

A smooth boyish face, framed by straight, blond hair, met her gaze. His stocky build reminded Sara of the farm boys in the Society. He smiled, and Sara was no longer afraid.

"My name is John Hamilton," he introduced himself, "and I must compliment you on how very well you danced with our host. One would almost think you two had practiced beforehand, especially

97

that new dance. I've never seen anything like it. What is it called?"

"It's a waltz. Dominic saw it on a recent trip to Germany. He feels it will become very popular."

"Without intending to embarrass you, may I say how very beautiful you are? I couldn't take my eyes off you."

Sara lowered her eyes beneath his scrutiny. "Thank you."

"I used to live here, years ago, and I don't remember any little girl who could have grown up to be the charming young woman you are."

The darkness covered Sara's blush, but strangely she felt no aversion to him, nor did he seem to be making untoward advances. His words were spoken with genuine interest in Sara as a person. She liked him.

"I'm not from Charlottesville," she told him freely. "My home is in Pennsylvania. I'm here visiting my sister-in-law."

"And who might that be?"

"Catherine Throne."

"You're related to Mrs. Throne? How marvelous."

"Do you know her?"

"Yes, indeed! I'm practically part of the family. Her husband Andrew was my mentor. I studied architecture with him years ago."

"Do you live around here?"

"No, I'm from Philadelphia. I have a firm there."

"Did you come to visit the Thrones?"

"Not specifically, although I certainly plan to do so at the earliest opportunity. I'm here on business."

"You must know Dominic, then, uh . . . Mr. Lansford."

"Yes. We grew up together."

Silently they looked up at the dazzling array of stars that filled the clear winter sky.

"Here we are," he spoke first, "old friends, and I don't even know your name."

"Sara Parsons."

"Well, Sara Parsons, where exactly in Pennsylvania did you live?"

"The northeast. I grew up in the Society."

"Ah, yes. I know of them. They have a good reputation for being hard workers and peaceable folk. Is this the first time you've been away?"

"Yes. I was reared by the Society and only came here to visit Catherine after my husband died. Simon was Catherine's brother."

"I see," John Hamilton said thoughtfully, "I hadn't known Mrs. Throne had a brother." Then, noticing her discomfort, he added, "I think we should get you inside, Sara. You're going to catch cold with only my coat to protect you from this December chill."

John held the door for her and Sara stepped into the ballroom, grateful for the rush of warm air which greeted her.

John removed his coat from her shoulders, allowing his hands to rest for just a moment on Sara's arms. She smiled her appreciation before her eyes drifted into the distance. Dominic was staring at her, scowling as though he had caught her doing something she oughtn't. With a defiant toss of her head, Sara turned back to John.

"Thank you for protecting me from the cold. You're very kind."

"It's imperative to be kind to a beautiful lady," he answered gallantly.

"Here you are!" called Catherine gaily. "Oh, and who is that with you? John Hamilton! Is it really you?"

"It is indeed, my dear Mrs. Throne."

Sara watched their warm greeting with interest.

"And you'll only be here for one week?" Catherine chided him, after he had told her the purpose of his visit.

He glanced at Sara. "Unless there is reason for me to stay longer."

Catherine caught the look and her eyes moved to Sara where she saw a flush rise to her cheeks. "You must come to dinner tomorrow night," she invited John. "I shan't take no for an answer."

"I would never refuse an invitation from you, madame. Your home has always been like my own."

"You are kind to say so, John. I only wish Andrew were alive to see you again and to learn how successful you are with your architecture. Now there are just Lydia and me."

"And Sara."

"Yes . . . Sara," Catherine beamed. "I see that you two have already met."

"It was my great pleasure." He bowed slightly toward Sara and she smiled shyly in return.

Catherine turned to introduce Sara and John to other guests who had stopped to speak with her, then Sara excused herself and wandered through the room, looking for Jane. On the way, there were lavish compliments and invitations to dance, but none of the young men danced with the subtle elegance of Dominic. And not one of them could have persuaded her to waltz—not even John Hamilton.

It was while she was conversing again with John that Jane Robertson burst upon them, so bubbly with joy that Sara stepped aside to hear her. John bowed gallantly and left them to chat.

"Sara!" Jane gushed. "I've been looking everywhere for you! You could not begin to guess what has just happened!" Her bright blue eyes sparkled in anticipation of sharing her news.

"Tell me, please," Sara begged, laughing a little at her new friend's exuberance.

"Dominic Lansford did ask me to dance, after all."

"Jane, that's wonderful!"

"And here's the best part." She leaned closer. "He asked me right in front of Lydia!" Without pausing, she plunged ahead. "You should have seen her face. She was livid. Oh, he is the most divine partner. But

100

honestly, Sara, I don't know how you ever managed to do that special waltz with him. Everyone is talking about it!''

Sara was suddenly reminded of Dominic's command to meet him in the library. She had no idea how much time had elapsed since she had first gone outside, but she was sure it must be over an hour. *Good*, she thought to herself, *let him wait forever!*

But then her wiser nature took over, reminding her of the times Dominic had been nice to her, and also calling to mind Catherine's lessons on social etiquette. Would she be unspeakably rude in not consenting to speak with her host?

But why should I, she argued with herself, *when he didn't ask me kindly, but told me, straight out, that I was being commanded to appear? I'm not going!*

More minutes passed and Jane continued to nibble at the delicious food while Sara merely walked beside her, distracted with the conflict raging within.

With a loud sigh, she finally turned to Jane.

"I'm sorry, but there's something I must attend to at once. Perhaps we'll get together later.'' She walked away in search of the library, and found a slave who directed her down the hall to the farthest room on the right. A tall-case clock with arched hood and brass finials began to chime the hour just as Sara arrived, breathless and apprehensive.

Thinking she was already late, Sara did not knock before opening the door, certain that Dominic was waiting for her. But when she stepped inside, she froze. Dominic was indeed there, but he was not at all aware of Sara's tardiness. He was completely absorbed—in kissing Lydia.

The two of them were standing near one of the windows. Startled at Sara's unwitting intrusion, they looked up, and Sara blushed scarlet, wishing she could suddenly become invisible. Dominic muttered an oath, and Lydia smiled, her pert just-kissed mouth turning up triumphantly at the corners.

"It's customary to knock before opening a closed door!" Dominic spit the words at Sara. "You're early."

"It's obvious I shouldn't have come at all!"

Dominic frowned at her saucy reply, and even Sara was surprised at herself. After all, why should she care what Dominic did? He was not required to answer to her. He could kiss every unmarried girl at his precious Winter Frolic if he wanted to!

She turned her back and started for the door, but a powerful hand gripped her arm. "We have things to discuss."

"You're busy."

"Lydia and I are finished."

"Dominic?" Lydia questioned.

"Later, Lydia. I have to speak to Sara."

"I don't see why," Lydia pouted, moving to Dominic's side with a coquettish look. "I think what we were discussing was infinitely more interesting than anything you could have to say to Sara."

"Do as I say, Lydia, and leave Sara and me alone." Dominic's tone was flat.

Lydia became all smiles and willing compliance.

"All right, Dominic, I'll go back to the party, but you must promise to join me as soon as you can." She slithered by him and touched his lips with one slender finger.

Dominic said nothing, but Sara glimpsed Lydia's smirk just before she pulled the door closed behind her.

CHAPTER 9

"THERE'S A REASON for what you saw," he said at last, his mouth taut and unsmiling.

"Really?"

"But we shall discuss that at another time."

"I see no reason to discuss it at all."

"Why were you so early?"

Sara paused before answering. "You make it sound as though I've committed a crime."

"I thought you would be late."

"Oh?"

"Because of your friend."

"Jane?"

"No. The good-looking man with the adoring eyes."

"Oh, you mean John Hamilton." Sara blushed with pleasure that Dominic had noticed the way in which John looked at her.

"He seems familiar to me."

"He used to live here, and was apprentice to Catherine's husband. He says you know each other."

"Ah, yes. He went north somewhere to become an architect."

"To Philadelphia."

"Mmm, well, I didn't call you here to talk of one of your admirers, of whom you seem to have many this evening. I want to discuss your staying with Catherine."

"I thought we had exhausted that subject."

"Not as long as you continue to resist reason."

"It isn't stubbornness that dictates I return to the Society, but obligation. Obligation to a family I care a great deal about, a family that lovingly took me in when my world with Simon collapsed. Please don't make me feel guilty for what I have to do."

Dominic's eyes were harsh. "So you can just walk away from all the kindness Catherine has shown to you?"

"It isn't easy. . . ."

"But you'll do it, just to return to that motley group of farmers who don't know what's going on in the world."

"Stop it!" Sara raised her voice to him. "I won't have you speaking disrespectfully of the Society!"

She turned toward the door, but Dominic stepped in front of her. "I'm not through with you."

Sara's eyes misted with tears. "Dominic, you're not being fair to me. I love Catherine. I've enjoyed my stay with her. But I can't live here forever. I have my own life. I want to go back."

"I don't think you really do." He leaned toward her. "I thought you wanted to learn about life. What about the things we discussed that day we were out in the carriage? Have you read the books I've recommended to you? And what about this?"

He reached out and pulled Sara into his arms, kissing her hard, crushing her against the steel tautness of his muscular body as his mouth demanded a response from her that she fought to suppress.

104

Sara knew he was angry and disgusted with her, and, therefore, was totally puzzled. Why was he kissing her? As she struggled to free herself, a strange thrilling sensation rose in her body, racing through her arms and neck and face, igniting her heart and nerves, leaving her dizzy.

Now that Jane had enlightened her, she had to prove to him that she was not one of those unprincipled women who enjoyed physical passion.

So she fought him, but she lost the battle. His manly domination over her tore away her last remaining shreds of dignity. Her hands, pushing against his chest in tight little fists of resistance, gradually opened and slowly moved up the granite hardness of his body, feeling the muscles in his arms and shoulders, finding their way around his neck and into the thickness of his dark hair.

He shuddered and the ferocity with which he held her suddenly gave way, amazingly, to tenderness. He brought his hands up and cradled her face between them and gently kissed her eyes, her forehead, her cheeks, the throbbing pulse at the base of her throat. Sara did nothing to stop him. She had seemingly lost all ability to maintain propriety.

Dominic lifted his head. His eyes swept her with a look she could not fathom.

She groaned. "Why are you doing this to me?"

An unpleasant smile curved the corners of his mouth. "Why not? You're not the only person who knows how to be cruel."

Abruptly he pushed her away from him and an angry glint flashed in his eyes. "Remember that," he snarled, "when you're back in your sanctimonious Society, and the nights are cold and there is no man to enfold you in his arms. And remember Catherine, a woman who has loved you, but whom you have no qualms about leaving."

He strode out of the room, leaving Sara to stare in agony at the open door.

She'd remember. Oh, yes! How could she ever forget? The searing impression of his mouth lingered like a torch on her lips, as did the shame of knowing that he had not kissed her because he cared for her. Quite the contrary. He had merely humiliated her by kindling her ardor and then abandoning her, just as he implied she had aroused Catherine's love and was now planning to forsake that love.

Sara felt empty and emotionally exhausted. Her self-respect was shattered. Dominic despised her for what he thought was selfishness. She was helpless to persuade him differently unless she stayed with Catherine, and she couldn't do that. The MacReadys needed her.

Tears fell upon her smooth pale cheeks as she stood, immobilized, staring at the open door.

To Sara's surprise, it was Lydia who stepped inside and closed the door.

"My, my," she purred, ignoring Sara's distress. "Whatever did you say to Dominic to make him so angry? I've never before seen such a hostile look on his face."

Sara brushed away her tears and could not begin to find the words to explain to Lydia what had just happened between herself and Dominic.

"Since you're not going to volunteer an answer," Lydia went on, strolling catlike around Sara, perusing her from narrowed piercing eyes, "I'll just have to guess. Then you can tell me whether or not I'm right."

Sara said nothing.

"Dominic is disgusted with you because he thinks you're ungrateful. Isn't that right?"

Sara did not agree or disagree.

"He feels you don't appreciate all that my dear mother has done for you since you came to visit us.

And he's right, of course. Dominic is very fond of Catherine, you know."

"Yes."

"And she of him. She has always hoped that Dominic and I will marry. And we will. She's a natural matchmaker, which is why it's no surprise that she asked Dominic's help in finding you a husband."

"What?" Sara gasped.

"Oh, didn't you know that my mother asked Dominic to create a new Sara—one more suitable for a wealthy husband of Virginia aristocracy?"

Sara's mouth dropped open. "I don't believe you."

Lydia laughed, a tinkling condescending laugh. "Oh, come now, Sara. Did you really think Dominic paid attention to you because he wanted to? My goodness, you *are* naïve. Dominic is one of the wealthiest, most intelligent, most sophisticated men in Virginia. He's highly respected. He sets political policy. He knows important people in government, including President Jefferson. Do you really think such a man could find you interesting, when he can have any woman he wants?"

She paused. "Oh, look at your face, you poor dear. You were flattered when he took you for a walk and carriage ride, weren't you? You thought he was personally attracted to you. But you must face facts, Sara. Dominic would never entangle himself with someone from the back country. Family connections and status mean everything to Virginians, Sara. Any woman who bears the proud name of Mrs. Dominic Lansford, I guarantee, will be a lady with an impeccable family background—not a little country girl who has no idea who—let alone *what* her parentage might be."

She smiled sympathetically. "Besides, you're far too religious for Dominic. He gave that up years ago, thank goodness. I think it's time you realized what your place is here. At the request of my mother,

Dominic agreed to teach you some of the aspects of being a fine lady. I heard them discussing it. It's as simple as that. Nothing more. Tonight. . . .''

A pathetic sob escaped Sara's throat. "Dominic asked me to dance because of a promise to Catherine?"

"But of course. It was the perfect occasion to show you off to all the eligible men of the county. The fact that Dominic Lansford seemingly finds you attractive only makes you that much more desirable to the others. Men do so love competition."

Fresh tears plummeted down Sara's cheeks. The gentle kiss Dominic had given her in the carriage had meant nothing to him. There had not been one ounce of true caring on his part in the love scene they had shared the first night he had tutored her. It had been only a momentary physical reaction on his part, and one he had never repeated . . . until tonight.

Sara's hand moved to her lips where she could still feel the rapture of Dominic's kisses. They had been tender and romantic—at least for her. Obviously, he had intended them as punishment for her stubborn insistence that she must leave Catherine and return to the Society. He had never even thought of her as a friend. All the times he had spent with her, even his choice of her as his partner tonight, had been done as a favor to Catherine.

Sara's humiliation at this revelation was even greater because Lydia had enlightened her. Lydia was all the things she was not: genteelly born, properly educated, with a respected mother and a father whose memory was revered. Sara's decidedly unimpeccable past included being abandoned by a father who thought more of some mysterious commitment than he did of caring for his infant daughter, and being raised by simple unsophisticated people who cared little for the wealth and politics of the outside world.

Of course she would not be a suitable wife for a

Virginia gentleman. It was perfectly understandable that Catherine would want to change her from an ugly unacceptable caterpillar into a delicate desirable butterfly. And who better to help with the transformation than a man of good breeding and intelligence, as well as appreciation of women? That man was Dominic Lansford.

Still, Catherine had known all along that Sara did not want to marry again. Both Catherine and Dominic had heard her declare this. Yet Dominic's aid had been enlisted—for the poor stupid girl who was not worthy to be anyone's wife.

How degraded she felt, to be trained like an ignorant dog or horse so she could be seen in public without bringing embarrassment to others.

Broken-hearted, Sara ran sobbing from the room, her self-confidence shattered. She fled down the great hall, wiping blindly at the tears that prevented her seeing where she was going. She, therefore, did not see the figure who caught her and held her firmly in his grasp.

Startled, she looked up. John Hamilton stared down at her in grave concern.

"Sara, whatever is the matter?"

Sara instantly felt his compassion. Gasping for breath, she could not find the proper words to explain what had just happened to her.

Silently, without making any demands for an explanation, he simply folded her gently in his arms and held her until her crying subsided. Thereby comforted, Sara relaxed at last and allowed his strength to sustain her, for she had none of her own.

"Do you want to go home?" he whispered into her soft shining hair.

"Yes, please," she whimpered softly. "But first I must find Catherine."

"I'll go with you."

"No. I need to speak to her privately. If you'll wait

for me here, I'll return as soon as I can." She gave him a weak little smile.

John nodded his assent and Sara entered the ballroom. Guests were laughing and chatting in congenial groups. Others were still on the dance floor, working up a hearty appetite for the elaborate meal that was soon to be served.

Sara threaded her way through the people, her face grim, her heart immune to their gaiety. Indeed, she walked woodenly, her whole body and soul numb to feeling.

When she found Catherine at last, Sara motioned to an unoccupied corner where they might talk.

"Sara, why are you crying?" Catherine gasped, peering with bewilderment into Sara's tear-stained face. "What has happened?" She reached for the girl's hands, but Sara pulled them away.

"Did you ask Dominic to tutor me so you could find me a husband?"

The words were as cold and incisive as the blade of a new knife; their cuts, as clean and sharp.

"Sara . . ." Catherine groped for the words.

"Tell me!" Sara demanded.

"Y-yes," Catherine admitted, "but, my dear. . . ."

Her words fell on empty air. Sara had already turned and was walking out of the room, her back straight, her head held high. She had the truth.

In the great hall she accepted John's arm around her shoulder. He led her toward the front door after tenderly placing her cloak about her stiff shoulders. Her eyes were glazed, unseeing; her silence, frightening. She did not say goodnight to Dominic who happened to come into the hall at that moment. She didn't see him. Neither did she see the look of challenge that flashed between Dominic and John Hamilton.

CHAPTER 10

SARA SLEPT FITFULLY THAT NIGHT, slipping in and out of consciousness, her mind awhirl with the events of the day. Throughout her dreams Dominic appeared, tall and handsome and commanding, gazing deeply into her eyes, dancing the waltz with her under the romantic shimmering light of the candles, holding her tenderly, the woman of his choice among all the beauties in the room.

Then Lydia would appear, laughing, ridiculing her with cruel words: "He's only doing it for Catherine. He's only doing it for Catherine."

Dominic echoed her words. "It's true," he would say, his eyes cold and heartless, "very true."

Sara woke with a start and sat up in the bed. She was shivering, and she rubbed her hands over her arms for warmth. It was still dark. The curtains at the barely opened window fluttered gently from the faint breeze drifting through the crack.

Sara rejected the temptation to creep back under the covers and escape again into sleep. She needed to think, even though thinking was painful. It brought back all sorts of ugly sordid memories. But she knew she must do something. It would soon be daylight and she would have to face Catherine. What could she say to her? How should she act? And then there would be the next inevitable meeting with Dominic. Whatever would she say to him?

The real humiliation was the fact that they—Catherine and Dominic—had discussed her and decided that, against her knowledge and will, she was to be molded and educated and recreated into a new person. This was the condition and reality that made it impossible for her to stay at Grand Oak for even one more day.

It was not that she thought of herself as perfect, without room for improvement. Far from it. She knew very well that she was not as well educated or socially minded as the wealthy people with whom Catherine and Dominic daily associated. Still, that didn't make her an unworthy person. What she was inside was more important than the number of books she'd read in her lifetime, or whether she could play the piano as well as Lydia, or if she wore the right clothes and could pick up the proper fork at dinner. Those were external things and shouldn't mean more than kindness and caring and being a hard worker and loving God, above all else, and wanting to serve and please Him. A man should respect her for that, not ridicule her.

Staring into the space of her room into the gray darkness that surrounded her with images both real and unreal, Sara tried to cope with the violent emotions that ripped at her heart and senses. She wanted to scream. She wanted to cry. She wanted to bury herself beneath the warm covers and never come out to face the world again. She wanted most of all never to have to see Dominic and Lydia and Catherine again.

All the hurt and confusion and shattered emotions

112

that raged through her trembling body and soul convinced Sara the one thing, the only thing she could do to preserve what semblance of self-respect she had left, was to leave this place, leave Catherine's house, leave the rolling gentle hills of Virginia, leave Dominic—all of them—and return to the Society. That was where she belonged. That was where she had always belonged.

Sara scooted to the edge of the bed. No tears stood now in her pale lifeless eyes. No expression of hate or disappointment or anguish now twisted her face; her features seemed carved from marble. She stood up, and her legs shook beneath her. Slowly, as if controlled by some force other than her own, she made her way to the elaborately carved armoire standing in one corner of her beautiful room. In the very back, buried behind the exquisite clothes Catherine had provided for her, Sara found the dilapidated cloth valise she had brought when she had first come to visit.

With cold trembling hands she stuffed into it the few paltry articles of clothing that were truly her own, save for what she was wearing. She walked out of the room, making her way silently down the stairs, staring straight ahead, oblivious of the very surroundings which, but a few days ago, had enthralled her with their beauty and richness.

But already she was, in her mind, no longer a part of this opulent society. She was going home, where people cared for her just the way she was.

She was Sara Parsons, Simon's widow. The title commanded respect, as did her name, which she had never done anything to sully. She had never before been ashamed of who she was, and she was not going to start now. She would go back to the humble shelter of the MacReadys' home, to the simple food they willingly shared with her, to the people of the Society who made up the only family she had ever known.

In the still, pale darkness of early morning, she opened the tall front door and walked through it, gently closing it behind her. She plodded down the smoothly raked pathway which led from the house through the sprawling yard to the main road.

Once at the gate, she did not even turn around to gaze once more at Catherine's home, where she had been happy until the events of last night had shattered forever her idyllic existence there.

She trudged down the normally soft and sandy road which now lay cold and hard beneath winter's frozen blanket. Magnificent Virginia magnolias stood gaunt at the sides of the road. The wild iris and columbine that ran rampant up the hills in the spring now lay dormant. Had all the trees been fully leafed and the flowers profuse in their brilliant colors, Sara would not have seen them.

A blast of cold air hit her and Sara shivered under the lightweight wool cloak she had grabbed from her armoire at the last moment. She had almost forgotten it, this flimsy garment she had brought with her from Pennsylvania, because it had lain behind the heavier, more attractive one Catherine had had made for her.

The full realization of what she was doing had not yet come to Sara. Walking from Virginia to Pennsylvania seemed, in her confused mind, as simple as walking to the house next door. Leadenly she placed one foot in front of the other, keeping her eyes straight ahead.

A sudden gust of wind whipped the ends of her dark blue cloak, but Sara scarcely noticed. Nor did she react when the first few drops of rain gently fell upon her hair and forehead. The murky sky, overcast with heavy dark clouds, dropped its moisture upon the earth and upon the runaway girl who plodded on, feeling nothing, not even the pain of leaving the two people she adored.

When Sara awoke she had no idea where she was. Her first conscious thought was that she was warm and that there was no chilling rain relentlessly beating down upon her. She was in a bed, covered by dry sheets and several thick blankets. She tried to think how she might have gotten there, but snatches of memory moved through her clouded mind. She saw herself struggling through the rain, falling, feeling pain, and then nothing until she felt strong arms around her and a distorted face peering into hers, and heard someone calling her, "darling."

She tried to change her position in the bed, but any movement brought discomfort, and she groaned.

Immediately a figure which had been reclining in a chair at the other side of the bed jolted to a sitting position.

"You're awake!" Dominic exclaimed. "Thank God!" and Sara beheld him in surprise as he leaned toward her, anxiety etched in every line of his handsome face. Sara's eyes darted nervously from one side of the room to the other and came back to settle on his weary face, knowing they were alone.

"Where am I?" she questioned weakly, trying to sit up a little, but finding herself unable to do so.

"At my home," he answered. "The Willows."

"But how. . . ?" She shifted wearily against the pillows supporting her head. At that moment, from somewhere deep within, she knew it had been Dominic who had held her and called her "darling."

He sat on the edge of the bed and gathered her hands into his. "Don't talk now. You need to rest— and eat. You must be starving. The doctor has been here and says we must take very good care of you if you are to recover properly."

"Recover from what?"

Sara struggled again to right herself in the bed, but Dominic's strong hands came down upon her shoulders, easing her back against the pillows. She shivered and coughed several times.

"You were out in the rain all night before I found you," he told her gently. He brushed a stray lock of hair from the side of her face. "Don't concern yourself with questions. You must eat, and drink liquids, and above all, rest. Doctor's orders. And my orders. I'm going to personally make sure they're carried out."

Dominic went to the table and returned with a dainty cup. He sat close to her and slipped his arm under Sara's shoulders, lifting her just enough so she could drink from the cup. She rested against the firm hardness of his chest, and relaxed, knowing she was safe as long as he was there. She sipped as much of the hot brown liquid as she could manage, and felt its healing warmth surge through her whole body. She groaned in pleasure.

"It's beef broth," Dominic told her. "Drink all you can."

Sara was so weak that only Dominic's strong reassuring arm around her enabled her to do so. She tilted her head back and looked up at him. His eyes had been formidable and harsh when they had beheld her in the library of his house. Now, surprisingly, they were tender and filled with great concern.

"Thank you," she whispered, and tears trembled in the corners of her eyes.

"Sara," he whispered, and his lips moved strangely. Then he held the cup to her lips again.

"Can you drink any more?"

"No. I'm sorry. You're very kind."

Dominic carefully eased her down onto the bed and put the half-empty cup on a nearby table. He picked up one of Sara's hands and raised it to his lips. "You're going to be just fine," he assured her. "I want you to sleep now. I'll be back later and we can talk."

116

Sara clutched his hand. "Dominic, don't leave me!" Her eyes were suddenly wild with fear and her grip surprisingly strong.

Dominic leaned closer. "Sara, I won't leave you. I promise. You're safe."

She sighed, exhausted even by that small effort. The room began to swim before her eyes and she did not know that Dominic held her hand until she fell asleep.

When Sara woke again, it was nighttime. The room was dark except for the soft glow of a small lamp coming from beside the bed. She still felt unbelievably weak, and her eyes slipped shut almost immediately. She thought she heard voices, though everything seemed very far away and she wasn't entirely sure if she were awake or dreaming.

"Pneumonia?" she heard a smooth female voice whisper. It sounded like Catherine. "How serious?"

"Very serious, I'm afraid," a man's anguished voice answered. Dominic. "If Sara lives through the next three to six days, she'll probably survive, but there is no way of knowing now." His voice seemed to break. "She can't be moved for at least three weeks, the doctor said. She must stay here. This room must be kept comfortably warm during the day, and ten degrees cooler at night. She's to have proper food, lots of liquids, wet compresses with stimulating liniments. . . ."

The violent sound of a fist being slammed into a palm broke the eerie stillness of the room. "Why did this have to happen?"

"You can't blame yourself, Dominic. It's really my fault. I shouldn't have urged her to stay here with me. I'll never forgive myself for not being more sensitive to her feelings."

The voices dropped to a whisper, but Sara had slipped into sleep again. A sense of peace enfolded her. Dominic and Catherine were here. They cared about her. Both of them.

Sara had no idea how many days passed in which she was only dimly aware of her surroundings. But one morning she awoke early and felt enormously better. Her head did not ache, nor did it feel damp or hot.

She looked around the room, appreciating its beauty for the first time. The chairs, tables, the carpet on the floor, the draperies at the windows—all spoke of fine taste inclined toward the masculine, and Sara pondered in awe that she was in Dominic's home. Excited, yet frightened at the thought of being so close to him, she remembered all too clearly his anger on the night of the Frolic.

"Good morning."

Sara looked up to see Dominic striding into the room. He came over to the bed and sat down in a large comfortable-looking stuffed chair. Her heart quickened at the sight of him. He was wearing a camel-colored riding coat, and tight-fitting breeches disappeared into sleek riding boots. Was it the broadness of his shoulders or the sure knowledge of powerful muscles that lay beneath the finely tailored clothes that thrilled her?

"How are you feeling?" he asked, his eyes drifting with genuine concern over her.

"Quite well, thank you."

"I'm glad to hear that."

"Dominic, I want to thank you. . . ." The words stopped in her throat as tears slid into her eyes and threatened to embarrass her by dropping onto her cheeks. "I want to thank you," she struggled on, "for finding me and saving my life."

"You're safe now. That's all that matters."

"No, that isn't all. I'm safe because of you. I didn't know where I was out there. I couldn't find any shelter and I was so very cold and wet, and the wind kept blowing. Then I tripped over something and wrenched my knee and couldn't walk." She began to cry.

He came to her in the bed, folding her hands tenderly in his. "You mustn't think about that now, Sara."

"But you found me, Dominic. You found me."

"Hello there," called a cheerful voice from the doorway. It was Lydia, dressed charmingly in a lovely green gown of frills and lace, discreetly buttoned to the neck, her fine red hair tucked into a lacy mobcap with tendrils charmingly escaping over her forehead and around her cheeks. She was holding a tray of food. Sara was surprised to see her.

"Cook said you wanted breakfast brought up to Sara, Dominic," she said sweetly.

Dominic looked at Sara. "Can you eat something, Sara?"

She gazed at him with huge eyes. "I'll try."

"Good girl."

Lydia glided across the room and set the tray down on a table beside the bed. She looked enchanting and Sara felt uncommonly ugly at that moment.

"Sara, dear," Lydia bubbled happily, "I'm so glad to see you're feeling better. You gave us all a fright, didn't she, Dominic? We wondered if you'd ever come back from the dead."

Dominic stood abruptly and gave Lydia a warning look. But she neglected to see it in her bustling about, smoothing Sara's covers and helping Sara to sit up. But Sara saw it and flinched. Had she been near death?

Lydia placed the food tray on her lap with great care. "There. You should enjoy your breakfast—bread and honey and two fresh eggs."

"Thank you, Lydia."

"Yes, thank you," Dominic added.

Lydia beamed cheerfully. "Why, Dominic, didn't you ask me to come and nurse Sara back to health, and didn't I say I would do anything, anything at all to see that she recovers? Why I don't mind changing sheets, applying poultices and wet compresses, bringing her food, keeping away visitors. Whatever it takes to make sweet Sara totally well, that's what I'll do."

"That's awfully good of you, Lydia," Sara said, ashamed of herself that she was not entirely thrilled to have Lydia hovering around.

"Why don't we leave Sara to eat in peace, Lydia?" Dominic suggested.

"All right. We can have our breakfast together, and I'll come back later and pick up Sara's tray."

"Good idea," he agreed. "Eat slowly, Sara, and only what you want. You mustn't shock your system with too much food too soon."

Sara's eggs cooled as she thought of being here—being cared for—in Dominic's house. Neither Dominic nor Lydia had chided her for running away, but sooner or later she would surely be asked to explain her reasons to Dominic. The thought of that confrontation filled her heart with dread.

Lydia breezed into the room some time later, her face radiant, her pretty eyes sparkling. Sara was sure the reason for that smile was Dominic. Lydia had made no secret of her adoration of him.

Lydia whipped the tray off Sara's lap. "My, my," she scolded gently, "you didn't eat your eggs, Sara, dear. The doctor says good food is important to your recovery."

"Recovery from what?" Sara only vaguely remembered hearing a conversation between Dominic and Catherine, but she couldn't remember clearly what they had said.

"Why, pneumonia. Didn't Dominic tell you?"

"No, he didn't. Was it really pneumonia?" A little flutter of fear invaded her heart. Many had died from pneumonia in the Society, though good health habits were always scrupulously observed.

"Yes, you poor thing. We didn't know whether you'd live or die after being out there in the forest all night. Why, it's a miracle you weren't attacked and eaten by a timber wolf or a fox or a panther. They're all over those woods, you know. Or you might have been bitten by a copperhead moccasin or a cottonmouth. They like to lie beside the roads in shallow ruts and surprise people. But here you are, on the mend, only you'll have to eat more than you did this morning if you want to regain your strength."

"I ate some of the bread."

"Oh, pooh! Only a nibble. I'm afraid I'll have to report you to Dominic. We had the loveliest breakfast together, he and I. Dominic is one of those marvelous men who is good-tempered in the mornings."

She pulled a straight chair close to one side of the bed. "It will probably take weeks to recover your strength, but don't you worry. I'm going to be right here for you. Whatever you want or need, you must let me know."

Sara could scarcely believe Lydia's concern for her, but the soft, lilting voice held no trace of hostility or condescension.

"Won't it be hard for you to come over here every day to take care of me?" she asked.

Lydia shook her head. "Oh no, Sara. Mother and I are staying here at The Willows. Dominic insisted on it, once the doctor told him you had to stay here and couldn't be moved back to Grand Oak. Dominic was a little put out, I can tell you. He's a busy man, you know, and hardly has the time to look after a sick person. And neither do his slaves. So Mother and I told him we'd relieve him of the burden and take care of you ourselves."

"How wonderful of you both."

Sara almost choked on the words. She knew she

was a burden to everyone, and that her escapade was causing a lot of trouble. Yet Lydia was being so nice to her. Had she misjudged her? Perhaps she was a genuinely caring person, after all.

"Lydia," she said, "I want you to know how much I appreciate your being here. I'd like for us to be friends, if we could."

Lydia smiled broadly. "Why, Sara, that's exactly what I've been thinking, too. I'm afraid we started off rather badly, but I'm going to make it up to you. I want to help you get well."

"And I want to get well, as soon as possible, so I can leave here. I don't want to be a hardship on Dominic any longer than is necessary."

"Don't worry too much about Dominic. Mother and I will soothe his ruffled feathers. He may be unhappy over having you here, but we're not going to have your health jeopardized by moving you too soon. The doctor said you must have lots of rest, and no excitement. You're still not entirely out of danger. Why, you almost died, Sara! But now that Mother and I are here, we're going to see that you are entirely well before we take you home, even if it takes weeks, or months."

Sara sighed unhappily. Poor Dominic. He had so skillfully covered up his true feelings about her being there. He had not seemed at all put out about it when he had spoken with her earlier, but she knew Lydia was right. Her illness *was* a burden to him.

Why was he always being called upon to help her? First, he had tried to teach her to be a fine lady. Then he risked his health by staying up all night searching for her in a torrential rainstorm. Now he had to endure her under his own roof, disrupting his life and that of his household. By now, he must surely wish she'd never come to Virginia.

"Sara, I'm going to find Mother now. She wants to see you. I must warn you that she is extremely upset about your running away. If she upbraids you too severely, you could have a relapse in your delicate condition. But she insists on seeing you. So, prepare yourself."

Lydia picked up the tray and walked to the door. "I'll be back after a while. Perhaps you'd like me to read to you. Dominic and I often read aloud to each other. 'Bye." She breezed out the door leaving Sara to contemplate the cozy scene Lydia's words brought to mind.

Lydia had only been gone for a few minutes when the doctor came in. Brusquely he examined Sara's eyes and throat, felt her pulse, asked her a number of questions, and left, saying nothing to her about her condition. Sara began to worry. Maybe she was not getting better, after all, and the doctor had not wanted to tell her. What if she were dying?

Catherine did come to visit, not at all upset with her, Sara thought. She was, instead, lovingly concerned.

"You're not to worry about anything, Sara. Dominic has generously offered to let you stay here as long as is necessary, and Lydia and I will do all we can to help."

Sara did not contradict Catherine, knowing as she did that Dominic actually had no choice but to allow her to recuperate in his home.

"Lydia has been very kind to me," Sara said. "She's offered to read to me."

"I'm glad she is being so thoughtful of you, dear."

An uneasy silence descended. Whereas they had always felt so comfortable in each other's presence, now there was an unspoken problem which had driven a wedge between them.

"Catherine, I'm sorry for all the trouble I've caused," Sara spoke first. "I know Dominic searched for me all night. . . ."

"Not only Dominic, but every male slave he could spare, as well."

"Oh, no!"

"Dominic is wonderful at such times. When Andrew died, it was Dominic who settled his affairs and provided comfort to me, even though he had had a tragedy in his own life not long before. He helped me through my grief and encouraged my struggle to go on with life."

Sara wondered what tragedy Dominic had endured.

"But you mustn't think of anything now but getting better," Catherine said with a loving smile. "And while you're doing that, remember how much you mean to me. When you're able to leave here, I'll arrange for you to be taken back to the Society."

"Oh, Catherine!"

When they fell into each other's arms, both wept tears of joy that they were together again, and Sara tried to pretend to herself that she was happy she would soon be going home.

CHAPTER 11

THE DAYS AND WEEKS PASSED and Sara grew stronger. She rested a great deal and ate whatever food was placed before her. She was cared for, even pampered. Every wish of hers, no matter how small, was fulfilled. Catherine was consistently kind and loving. Lydia was conscientious in her nursing duties.

Though Dominic made only infrequent visits, Lydia had already warned her how busy he was, so Sara was not surprised.

Lydia, however, reported to Sara every detail of the many hours she and Dominic spent together.

"Dominic is always praising me for my nursing skills," Lydia told her. "He says this is a whole new side of me he had not known existed."

She clasped her hands together and her beautiful green eyes drifted up to the ceiling where they gazed, dreamlike and unseeing, at the exquisite carved squares it had taken someone hundreds of hours to sculpt.

"I think Dominic is falling in love with me, and it's all because of you, Sara. Your being here has allowed me to spend more time with him than ever before. He sees me now as a woman he can admire. I hope you'll understand and forgive me if I thank you for running away and creating this whole delightful situation. I know it's been terrible for you—being so sick —then having to stay here when you know how badly Dominic thinks of you. I'm truly sorry for all that, but because of it, Sara, I've found the man I'm going to marry.''

She sighed with the wonder of it all, and leaned close to Sara. ''Can you keep a secret, Sara?''

''Of course.''

''I've been in love with Dominic ever since I was a child. He's always been so incredibly dashing and exciting to me. Perhaps because he's older and so sure of himself and so terribly in control of every situation. No other man I know can compare to him. I tried to make him notice me, but until these past few days he saw me only as the young daughter of a good friend. He never knew the real Lydia.'' She smiled. ''Now he does. Oh, Sara, I'm so happy. So very, very happy.''

She stood up and hugged herself, her face wreathed in a dazzling expression of love that Sara could not help envying. She suddenly bent down and kissed Sara's cheek.

''Thank you, Sara. Thank you, thank you. I'll never forget you for this. When you return to the Society, you must always remember that I adore you and am eternally grateful to you for having brought Dominic and me together.'' She paused. ''Perhaps we'll name one of our children after you when we get married and start a family.''

The very thought of Dominic's child—and Lydia's—being named after Sara left her speechless.

''You will be returning to the Society soon, won't you?'' Lydia asked.

''I think so.''

At that moment Sara became aware someone was watching her. She glanced up toward the door, at first seeing no one. Then her eyes dropped to a familiar face, peeking curiously at her from around the corner of the doorframe. It was Lizzie, an adorable three-year-old black child who had the largest, roundest eyes Sara had ever seen. She had been coming every day lately to stare at the beautiful lady in the bed, but each time Sara had called out to her, the child had fled.

Lizzie was an orphan, like Sara. Her mother had died of smallpox two years before and, supposedly, no one knew who her father was.

Sara's heart went out to Lizzie, not only because they shared a common lot in life, but because the little girl was uncommonly adorable. Her huge brown eyes stared at Sara as though Lizzie thought she would evaporate in a puff of smoke before her. Yet she could not be persuaded to enter the room, and Sara had never seen her smile.

Today a miracle happened. When Sara called out gently to Lizzie, the child hesitantly stepped inside the door where she stood stock still, holding her breath, her little chest puffed out, her eyes growing even larger as she listened to Sara's pleas to come closer and talk with her.

"What are you doing here, you naughty girl?" Lydia berated the youngster when she saw her. "You don't belong here!"

Lizzie gulped, then turned and fled. Sara sighed in disappointment.

"You mustn't encourage her, Sara," Lydia chided her. "She's not supposed to be in this part of the house."

But a few hours later, when Lydia was nowhere around, Lizzie came back. After much cajoling from Sara, Lizzie edged her way into the room, stopped at

127

the foot of the bed, and examined with intense interest the woman lying there.

"Lizzie, please come to me. I'd like to get to know you. I'd like to be your friend."

Sara held her breath as the child advanced slowly, then amazed her by gingerly climbing up on the covers, close enough for her to reach out and touch her. She did not do so, though, for she was afraid that any such move would frighten the child away.

Lizzie was dirty, her hands soiled from some food recently eaten, and a crust of dirt on both chubby legs. But it didn't matter to Sara. The child was beautiful to her, and totally acceptable, dirty or not.

Sara's eyes traveled up and down the healthy plump body of the three-year-old, thinking how much she reminded her of her favorite MacReady child. There was the same curious expression in the eyes of both children, the same cherubic wide-eyed innocence, the same puffy mouth, open and rounded, as though that position made it easier to evaluate the object of her interest.

With one stubby forefinger, Lizzie touched Sara's arm which lay exposed above the covers. Sara silently allowed Lizzie's exploration. Finally she turned her arm over, exposing her open hand. Instinctively, the child placed her small one in the palm of Sara's hand, and Sara's fingers closed gently over it.

Sara was delighted and smiled broadly but did not elicit a smile from Lizzie in return. Still, the child did not run away. She sat there, motionless, allowing her hand to be held by the white lady. Her eyes darted over Sara's facial features with such intensity it was as though this was the very first face she had ever beheld.

A sound at the doorway caused Sara to look up. Dominic was leaning against the frame, his arms folded across his wide chest, one long leg bent at the knee, the toe of his boot resting on the floor. He was watching the scene with amused interest. How long had he been there?

Lizzie noticed the change immediately, and jerked her little head around to see what the distraction was. When she saw her master, she gasped and jumped down from the bed and scurried as fast as her fat little legs would take her to escape through the door. But Dominic caught her and scooped her up in his arms.

"Not so fast, my little princess. You don't have to run away just because I'm here. It's perfectly all right for you to visit the nice lady."

Lizzie's head was bowed and she would not look at him, but she didn't squirm. She seemed to like being held thus. *And why not?* Sara thought. The poor child had no parents of her own. Were the other slaves kind to her, or did they treat her as an outcast? Sara planned to find out.

Dominic put the child down and she dashed along the hallway, nearly falling down the stairs in her haste to get away.

Both Sara and Dominic laughed. He came over to the bed and looked down at her.

"I've never seen Lizzie that bold before," he said, scrutinizing her with almost the same intensity as had the little girl. And was there a trace of admiration in them, too?

"She's adorable. It's taken every ounce of patience I have not to reach out and try to take her into my arms. Is she unhappy?"

Dominic thought a moment. "Perhaps. She goes from family to family, sleeping and eating where she will, and although no one shuts her out physically, they don't take her into their hearts. She belongs to everyone, and to no one."

"Isn't there anyone to love her? Grandparents, perhaps?"

"No. I'm sure Lizzie has never felt loved, or even wanted."

"I'd like to love her."

His gaze softened. "I'm sure you would. You sound like my mother who loved all the Negroes and treated them as if they were her very own family. Slavery was a part of her life, but she never whole-heartedly supported it." His eyes grew misty with the recollection. "In fact," he went on, staring across the room at nothing in particular, "I'm beginning to wonder if she was right in questioning why one race should be slave to another."

Sara sat very still, caught up in Dominic's train of thought. She remembered the warning from Catherine that Dominic didn't like to be questioned about his family, so she said nothing.

"About Lizzie . . ." Dominic cleared his throat and reached for a straightbacked chair which he turned to sit astride, his arms laced across the back. "She'd be most fortunate if you gave her the attention she has been denied. But let me caution you to think of her— if she forms a strong attachment for you, it will break her heart if she loses you."

Sara sighed. "You're right. But I can't turn her away. She's so tiny—so vulnerable," she mused, recalling her own sad circumstances.

"The doctor is very pleased with your progress and says you can soon go home," Dominic changed the subject.

Sara's eyes widened as her thoughts tangled in confusion. Dominic sensed her turmoil.

"Where is home, Sara?" he asked, not unkindly.

Catherine had promised to see that Sara was returned to the Society, but recently, whenever Sara had thought of going home, it had always been Catherine's house she had thought of.

"Which brings us to the reason you ran away."

Dominic's voice was firm and his eyes very grave. Sara had known he would eventually ask that question. What could she say to him? How could she

130

explain the feelings that had driven her? No clear explanation had come to her. Now there was no more pondering to be done. He wanted an answer. The directness of his gaze told her that plainly.

"Why?" he prompted her.

"It's hard to explain."

"I don't see why. Were you a prisoner at Catherine's? Would she have refused to let you go back to your people if you had really insisted? Had she mistreated you so badly that you had to sneak away from her in the middle of the night without so much as a thank-you, or at least the courtesy of an explanation?"

The words were spoken steadily, but there was censure in them.

"Catherine thinks it's her fault," he said, his eyes probing Sara's, "because she urged you to stay with her and not return to the Society."

"That wasn't the reason!" Sara burst out with the truth. "It was because she secretly asked you to prepare me for marriage."

"Where did you get that silly idea? Catherine asked only that I be your friend."

"So you took me for a walk and ride in your carriage because Catherine asked you to?"

"Partly."

Sara stared down at the covers. "I thought you did it because you liked me."

"I did like you . . . I do like you."

"And the books you wanted me to read were not part of a grand plan to take stupid Sara and make her more intelligent so she would become marriageable?"

Dominic frowned. "You have a vivid imagination, Sara. Catherine thought you wanted to learn, and so did I."

"I did, but not so I would be good enough to marry a Virginian."

Dominic stood up, his patience with her obviously

at an end. "Maybe that's not such a bad idea," he taunted. "I think you need a husband to help you to grow up and to teach you how to be a woman."

Sara gasped. "I've had a husband, thank you. And I know how to be a woman."

"Do you?" The derisive tone of Dominic's voice reduced Sara to tears. That he should think of her as a silly child broke her heart.

"Come, come," he admonished, "your tears may have turned John Hamilton into your quivering slave, but it won't work with me. You're the one to blame for this unfortunate incident. If you had really wanted to go back to the Society, you could simply have told Catherine and she would have arranged it. But you delayed your leaving and what else was she to think but that you really wanted to stay? She wanted to help you. You're barely more than a child. You're innocent and vulnerable and need someone to take care of you."

"I'll be twenty in a few weeks! I'm a grown woman and I don't need a man to take care of me!" Sara's voice rose higher with each punctuated statement.

"Rubbish!" Dominic snapped back at her, his voice rising, too. "You're selfish and immature! To me, those characteristics are the mark of a child."

"I am *not!*"

"What's going on here?" Catherine exclaimed, hurrying into the room. "I could hear you two shouting clear down the hall. Dominic, what have you been saying to Sara? She's in a state."

"Just things that needed saying, Catherine. Now that I've said them, I feel better."

Sara got up on her knees in the bed and pointed a finger at Dominic. There were no more tears in her eyes. Now she was angry. Her eyes danced furiously and her pretty rounded chin quivered.

"You think you know everything about women,

132

Dominic Lansford, but you don't. At least not about *this* woman!''

Dominic laughed. ''At last—some spunk. I was getting tired of the sanctimonious grieving widow. Thank goodness, you're over that phase.''

''Oooh!'' Sara screeched. She picked up a pillow and hurled it at him. He caught it and laughed more heartily. Sara threw the other and hit him squarely in the mouth. His head bobbed back in surprise and Sara applauded in triumph.

''Sara! Dominic!'' Catherine pleaded.

Dominic left the room, roaring with laughter.

Sara sank down on the bed and pounded the blankets with her fists. She could never recall being so angry. The sound of Dominic's laughter echoing down the hallway incensed her further.

''I don't understand you two at all,'' Catherine muttered. She left the room, shaking her head in disbelief.

Sara got off the bed and retrieved the pillows. She plumped them up and arranged them in place, then sank back into them and tucked her cold feet under the covers.

She was not tired. All the effort of arguing with Dominic had not hurt her. Instead, it had stimulated her. To her surprise she felt amazingly well. Wonderful, in fact. Excitingly alive. She must be getting better.

She smiled and stretched, feeling a delicious sensation flow through her arms and legs. She decided to get up and get dressed. She had spent enough time in bed.

Lydia came in just as she was trying to tug on a lovely mustard-yellow silk dress, one of two Catherine had had brought over from Grand Oak, but which had hung unused in a room that connected to the bedroom.

"Why, Sara darling, you're up. Here, let me help you with that dress."

Sara whirled on her. "I can do it myself, Lydia. I'm not a helpless child, you know."

Lydia stepped back a pace or two. "No . . . I guess you're not. What's the matter?"

"Nothing, Lydia. Nothing at all."

With an impatient tug, she yanked the dress over her head and shoulders. They both heard the awful sound of fabric ripping.

"I don't know why you're in such a snit," Lydia commented dryly, "but that's no reason to ruin a beautiful dress."

"Sorry," Sara grumbled.

Lydia stood back with her arms folded across her chest and watched Sara awkwardly arrange the dainty ruffles at her elbows and fluff the skirt so that it hung straight, the elaborate embroidery along the bottom hem almost touching the floor below Sara's bare feet.

"You'd better put some shoes on," Lydia warned her. "The floor is cold."

Sara turned on her. "I told you, I'm not a child. My feet are not cold. The floor is not cold. I may decide to go barefoot the rest of my life!"

Lydia gasped. "Fine. Fine. Good heavens, Sara, I've never seen you like this. Is this the real you or was the other Sara the true Mrs. Parsons?"

Sara glared at her, recalling Dominic's stinging words about being glad she was over the phase of being the sanctimonious grieving widow. Did he understand her better than she did herself? Was she really not the simple, quiet, unassuming Sara she and everyone else had thought?

She turned to Lydia. "I'm sorry, Lydia. Please forgive my outburst. I just had an unfortunate run-in with Dominic."

"Really?" Lydia's eyes sparkled with interest.

"A rousing argument would more aptly describe it. And then I threw two pillows at him. . . ."

"You did what?"

"Your mother must think we have both taken leave of our senses. But Dominic laughed at me, Lydia, and called me a child, and said other things that I just couldn't tolerate."

"My, my, my. How unkind of him."

"He's so certain he knows how everyone should live."

Lydia turned away from Sara, a sly smile turning up the corners of her pretty mouth.

"Don't worry about him, Sara. His opinion doesn't really matter to you, does it? After all, he's not someone you care at all about."

Sara sighed. "You're right. I certainly don't care what Dominic thinks about me. I know I'm not as selfish or immature as he insists I am."

"Of course you're not." Lydia turned around. "Would you like me to read to you, Sara?"

Sara studied Lydia's lovely face and then said, "I don't think so. Maybe later."

When Lydia left, Sara sat down in a chair and began to stare out the window at the bleak December day, contemplating what a mess she had made of her life. Dominic was disgusted with her. Catherine must feel she had not been appreciated. The MacReadys would sorely be missing her and wondering why she hadn't returned. Sara could not believe she had been in Virginia for a month. It seemed a lifetime. Her thoughts meandered through all the things that had happened to her there.

The charming sounds of an expertly played harpsichord drifted up from the downstairs and Sara listened to the music, wishing she could play. When a young woman came in with her dinner, Sara asked her, "Who's playing downstairs, Delia?"

"Miz Lydia, ma'am. Masser Dominic's lis'nin' real

close. He likes dat music. His mama. . . ." She stopped, leaving Sara to surmise that she had thought better than to betray information best left unspoken.

But Sara urged her on. "Please tell me about Mr. Lansford's mother, Delia. Did she also play the instrument?"

"Yes'm. She played it real good. Ever' day. An' her daughter, too."

"Her daughter? I didn't know Mr. Lansford had a sister."

"Oh, yes'm. 'Bout ten years younger 'n him. She was a pretty thing and Masser Dominic adored her." Delia tilted her head and surveyed Sara. "She looked a lot like you, ma'am, all young 'n' fresh 'n' fair-headed. But she was spunky. Oo-ee, did dat chile have a temper. She always got her way, too, 'cause she were de apple of her daddy's eye. Masser Dominic tried to straighten her out, but it di'nt do no good. She done run away an' no one knew where she was fo' de longest time."

"Did they ever hear from her again?"

"Yes'm. One day she up an' write 'em dat she was with some religious folk in Ohio. She liked it real well dere an' wanted to stay, but her folks an' Masser Dominic wanted her home, so they all went to bring her back."

Sara thought she would go mad waiting for the woman to continue with the story, but Delia didn't seem disposed to do so.

"So what happened?" Sara finally had to ask. "Did they find her and bring her home?"

"Oh, dey found Miz Claudia all right, but she done refuse to come back here. Said she liked it better where she was at. Said she liked readin' de Bible 'n' such. Her mama 'n' papa couldn't budge 'er. Den, on de way home, a terrible accident happened. De buggy tipped over and rolled down a steep hill and Masser Dominic's folks was killed. He was only bruised."

136

Sara groaned. "It must have been terrible for him."

"It were. He went into a rage. Day after de buryin', he rode straight back to Ohio to drag his sister home, whether she wanted to come or not. But she run away from him an' he couldn't find her. So he come back home all bitter 'n' angry inside. He was in a terrible fury fo' a long time, ma'am. No mo' sister. No mo' mama and papa. He stopped going to de church. Den Miz Catherine's husband died, an' Masser Dominic helped her, and dat's when he begin to come out of his deep sadness."

Delia murmured something about having to help in the kitchen, and scurried out the door.

Sara ate her supper, thinking about Dominic and his sister and the tragic loss of his parents. Now it was clear to her why he was so adamantly opposed to the Society. His sister must have lived with a similar group. Naturally he blamed them for having broken up his family. Sara's heart went out to him as she understood his grief.

It was strange, she thought, but he and she were in similar circumstances. He had no family, and neither did she. He, of course, had many friends, an important place in this community, and wealth. Still, he must yearn for the parents that had been denied him. At times in her life, she had longed desperately to know who her mother and father were and to have, just once, her parents hold her in their arms. But it had never come to be. She was alone, as Dominic was alone.

The room was dark. The night had captured the sky and Sara grew cold. She had been sitting in the chair for hours. The house seemed uncommonly still. Had everyone gone to bed already?

She stood up, feeling stiff, then stretched her arms and legs and turned her head from side to side. Glancing in the mirror, she saw that her hair was untidy, large bunches of it having fallen away from the holding combs. Taking the combs and pins out, Sara vigorously brushed her hair until it was smooth, but, too tired to put it up again, she left it down.

She walked around the room, feeling restless even after washing her face with water from a pitcher near the window.

I'm going downstairs, she decided. *I've been in this room long enough.*

With a lightened heart she walked to the stairway and began her descent.

CHAPTER 12

HALFWAY DOWN THE STAIRS Sara heard hearty laughter coming from the dining room. The door was closed, which was why she had not heard the sounds upstairs. Frightened lest she be discovered, Sara froze.

Dominic must have visitors. Undecided whether or not to proceed or return to her room, but too excited at this first venture, Sara decided to go on. She would stay as far away from the dining room as possible and only stay downstairs for a few minutes.

With cautious step she continued on, running softly down the hallway toward the one room she hoped would be safe for a while—the library.

Memories of her last visit there flooded her mind, but things were very different now. There would be no encounter tonight with Dominic. He was busy entertaining friends and would never know she had been there.

She carefully opened the door and went inside. The room was bathed in soft light from several oil lamps. Slowly Sara walked from one side of the room to the other, relishing the quiet, her fingers tracing an imaginary line along the cool smooth wood of several tables, her eyes delighting in the lovely fabrics of the furniture and draperies.

The room had an imposing personality of its own, as though the accumulated knowledge in the shelves and shelves of books that graced the south wall made it special among rooms.

What must it be like, Sara pondered, *to live in a house like this; to know that such a room as this exists to be enjoyed whenever one desires?*

She wondered if the wealthy people who lived in the grand Virginia homes truly appreciated them. If they had lived in such conditions all their lives, she doubted it, for she had come to believe that only one who has done without can truly appreciate fine possessions.

Sara wandered to the bookshelves. Her hand reached out and touched one or two volumes. She leaned closer to read the titles, but the light was too dim. She sat on the sofa, relaxing a moment, enjoying the peace. Then she noticed some objects on a nearby table, the most intriguing of which was a small box with an exquisite tapestried lid. It was old, but not worn. Her fingers moved along the smooth surface of the gold metal until they came to a clasp. When she pushed it, the lid popped up and a lovely little melody began to play.

The sudden sound in the very quiet room startled Sara and she slammed the lid shut. But she was fascinated with the dainty music box and in a moment lifted the lid again, confident that the people down the hall laughing and conversing in the dining room could never hear so quiet a sound.

The little melody played on and on, and Sara found herself swaying to its delicate rhythm. Her head tilted back, her eyes half closed, she moved rhythmically, savoring the peaceful moment.

140

"Put that down! Immediately!"

The command came from the door and Sara whirled around, almost dropping the music box in her surprise, her eyes wide with fright.

Looming in the frame of the door, the light from the hallway shining behind him, stood Dominic, tall, imposing, and at that moment, very angry.

"Did you hear what I said?"

He strode across the room and ripped the tiny instrument from her hand. For a moment he gazed at it, then put it back on the table. He glared at Sara.

"What are you doing here? You're supposed to be in bed." The words were hurled at her, like a physical assault.

"I . . . I wanted to get out of the room for a while. It's been such a long time."

"The doctor hasn't given his permission for that."

The coldness in his voice frightened Sara, as did his strange reaction to her touching the music box.

"I feel fine. I'm sure the doctor wouldn't mind my getting up. I won't be able to walk at all if I don't exercise my legs."

"And you'll be back in bed with a cold if you don't get something on your feet."

"My feet?"

Sara looked down and was horrified to see that she was wearing no shoes.

Without another word, Dominic scooped her up in his arms.

"Put me down!" she demanded.

"Gladly." Swiftly he carried her to the sofa where he unceremoniously dumped her on the green velvet cushions.

"Oh!" she cried out, trying to get up. But strong hands held her down. "Either sit there with your feet tucked under you to keep them warm, or I'll carry you upstairs to bed!"

Sara grumbled under her breath, but agreed reluctantly. She didn't want to go back to her room yet.

Dominic sat down beside her. "Now that I know what a temper you have, I'll have to be more careful."

Sara looked shocked. "I don't have a temper."

"As I recall, you threw some pillows at me."

"You deserved it."

"Did I?" He was smiling now. "You know, you amazed me. I had no idea you could be so feisty."

"I've never known anyone who could aggravate me so much!" Sara snapped.

Dominic chuckled softly, and his eyes traveled over the long luxurious hair flowing around her head and shoulders. "You really were quite a woman," he grew serious, "with your eyes flashing and your body tensed for battle." He leaned closer to her until she could see her own reflection from the oil lamps in his dark brown eyes. "Actually breathtaking," he added, raising his hand to play with a wayward curl which fell across the milky curve of her cheek.

Sara was spellbound by his look, but she struggled to break the romantic mood. "My anger was not intended to entertain you, Mr. Lansford."

"Ah, but I was entertained, Sara. You are a woman of fire and spirit. It was a part of your nature I had no idea existed."

"That was not the real me."

"I think it is. You're changing, Sara. You're facing new situations, experiencing new emotions everyday. You want to run away from them, but you can't. There's nowhere to hide from your own feelings."

Sara knew he was right, and the truth of his words worried her. She wasn't at all sure she could successfully handle the confusing emotions she felt when she was around him.

"I'm keeping you from your guests," she said.

"Yes," he agreed, but made no move to rise.

142

Sara didn't know what to say. She looked down at her hands, which were trembling. Slowly Dominic picked them up, turned them over, and kissed each palm, his lips igniting tiny exquisite sparks wherever they touched her skin.

"I thought I understood you completely after the first time I met you," he said caressingly, his eyes soft. "You were uncomplicated then. But now you're becoming a fascinating woman."

Sara held her breath and gazed at him, knowing she loved him. The sound of singing was heard in the hallway, a rich plaintive melody unlike anything Sara had ever heard before.

"The slaves," Dominic explained, without taking his eyes from Sara's face. "Tonight begins their week-long holiday from hard work. At midnight a cowbell will call them to a special worship they call 'Watching for the Coming of Christ.' They'll tell the Christmas story and sing for hours."

"I have lost all track of time! This is Christmas Eve?"

Dominic sighed and leaned back against the sofa, releasing her hands. "My guests are here for Christmas Eve dinner. Shortly we'll hang up the stockings for the children."

He reached behind him and picked up the music box Sara had been so entranced with before. He held it out to her. "I'd like for you to have this, Sara."

Hesitantly she took the box from his hands, her fingers inadvertently touching his skin. Scarcely breathing, they looked into each other's eyes.

"It seems special to you," she whispered.

"It was my mother's."

"I can't take something that belongs to your family. You must keep it." She tried to give it back to him, but Dominic's hands closed around hers.

"I want you to have it. I remember what delight it gave my mother. She'd be happy knowing it now

143

belonged to someone who felt about it the way she did. Forgive my boorish behavior earlier.''

Sara gazed into his face. Almost of their own accord, her fingers gently caressed the firm line of his jaw.

"You must have loved her very much," she said.

"Yes. But loving is too painful. When it's gone, there's nothing to take its place.''

"Except more love.''

He moved quickly, burying both his broad strong hands in the richness of her thick loose hair. He kissed her fiercely, then pulled back, devouring her with his eyes, before kissing her more tenderly as the music of the carolers drifted away into the night.

"I want to love you, Sara," he whispered, his voice husky and apologetic, "but I can't.''

Sara pulled herself out of his arms and stared at him, "Then don't love me. I didn't ask you to. I never expected it.'' She stood up.

Dominic stood, too. "Sara, let me explain.''

"There's nothing to explain. I've been through this before. I should have known it was coming. At least you have touched me tenderly. Simon never. . . .'' Her voice trailed off.

Dominic grabbed her fiercely by the shoulders. "What were you going to say?''

"It isn't important.''

Sara's eyes widened. She had let slip something she had vowed never to tell to anyone, ever.

Dominic shook her a little. "Were you going to say Simon never touched you?''

"Leave me alone," Sara pleaded. She burst into tears and tore herself from Dominic's grip, running toward the door of the room. But he caught her and whirled her around to face him.

"Tell me about Simon," he demanded. His nostrils were flaring, his eyes, angry orbs.

Sara sobbed and seemed almost to collapse in his

embrace. "I know there's something wrong with me that makes you unable to love me," she said in a pitifully small voice. "Simon didn't love me, either That's why he never touched me."

Simon stared at her in disbelief. "Sara, you can't mean that. You were married to Simon for six months."

"It's true. I'm not sure what I expected when I married him," she began in a singsong voice, barely aware of what she was saying. "No one ever spoke to me about it, but I knew something had to happen to make babies. I wasn't worried that I was so ignorant, because Simon was older, and had been married before, and had fathered a child. I knew he would explain everything to me. But he didn't. He didn't take me in his arms. He didn't say sweet things to me or try to kiss me. I was bewildered and then humiliated. I knew it had to be because of me that he didn't want me."

Dominic groaned. "Sara, listen to me. There's nothing wrong with you."

"Really? Then you must not be able to love me because I'm that other kind of woman."

"What other kind of woman?"

"Jane Robertson told me there are two kinds of women: the kind a man marries, and the kind he just . . . just toys with. I must be the kind he toys with because that's what you're doing with me. And it's because I let you know how much I enjoy it when you hold me and kiss me that you don't respect me. Jane says that a lady must never let a man know she enjoys such things, but you know how thrilled I am whenever you touch me. I'm so ashamed," she babbled on, "so ashamed that I'm that kind of woman."

Dominic pulled her fiercely into his arms and buried his face once more into the sweet-smelling luxuriance of her hair.

"Sara, listen to me! If Simon never made love to you, it was his own fault—not yours."

"No, Jane was right. There are two kinds of women. . . ."

"Forget about Jane! Sara, please sit down and let me explain some things to you."

"You don't need to explain anything. I understand it now. But I'm a lady, Dominic. I really am."

A great sob escaped her throat. It was so humiliating that to Dominic, of all people, she had told the awful truth about her marriage. She had made a fool of herself by doing so, and for letting him know how she felt about him. Was there no end to her stupidity?

"Leave me alone, Dominic! Leave me alone!"

She ran, crying, from the room, and didn't even notice Lydia pressed against the wall in the hallway, having heard everything, her face portraying quiet victory.

CHAPTER 13

CHRISTMAS DAY. How could Sara think of celebration, after the trauma of the night before? She had done a lot of thinking. Dominic's refusal to love her, for whatever reasons, must be best for her. His belief in God was not as deep as her own; his way of life, totally different. What she had thought was love for Dominic was nothing more than a strong fascination for a man who was unlike any other she had ever known. All kinds of problems would ensue if they allowed themselves to love each other.

Catherine reported that the doctor had said she could go back to Grand Oak tomorrow, if she would promise to rest there a week or so before returning to the Society.

"Is that still what you want?" Catherine asked her gently.

"It is," Sara assured her, but without much conviction in her voice.

"But we're going to stay here today and celebrate Christmas with Dominic," Catherine said. "He asked

147

me to invite you to share any part of the day, or all of it, with us if you feel up to it."

"Yes, thank you, I will."

Thirty guests and a dozen children of all ages came to breakfast. Across the bountiful table Sara was able to look Dominic in the eye without flinching or crying, or being haughtily angry for his rejection. All her quiet moments had enabled her now to accept the fact that she and Dominic did not belong together.

Afterward, they all went to church. The pews, festively decorated with evergreen, looked like arbors. Walking down the aisle toward the Lansford pew, Lydia slipped her arm through Dominic's, but he carefully removed it and gave her a look of reproach. Lydia pouted through the entire service, while Sara pretended not to notice and found herself greatly enjoying the reading of the Holy Scriptures and the sermon of the morning. The minister was a good speaker, but not as eloquent as Elder Johns of the Society.

Back at The Willows, Sara changed from the simple walking dress she had worn to church to a stunning pale blue flowered gown that Catherine said would be more appropriate for the day's celebration. Sara did not hurry through her dressing, for she knew there would not be very many more days when she would be able to wear such clothes.

She stood in front of the mirror gazing at the elegantly attired woman, and tried to still the heavy beat of her heart that told her she really did not want to leave Dominic's house tomorrow. Trying not to think of the fact that she very likely would never see him again, she fluffed the overdress of blue satin which opened down the front of her gown to reveal an underdress of silk. She eyed the square neckline edged with a narrow frill of lace, and fingered the puffed sleeves. She turned nearly around, listening to the soft rustle of the skirt and, looking over her shoulder, pondered the short train that would glide along the floor when she walked.

What would the people of the Society say if they could see her now? she wondered. What would the MacReadys think?

If Sara had been truthful with herself, and she had always tried to be, she would have had to admit that she loved the glamorous clothes she had been privileged to wear during her visit with Catherine. She had long since come to believe that there was nothing wrong with having the world's possessions, as long as they did not occupy a more important place in one's heart than the Lord.

While lying in bed, recuperating from her pneumonia, she had had time to think about that. She had even discussed it with Catherine who, it turned out, was very wise in spiritual matters. She led Sara to a new awareness of what it truly meant to love and serve God, and trust Him.

"Jesus said, 'I am come that they might have life, and that they might have it more abundantly,'" Catherine had told her one day. "If we don't have faith to accept His abundance, whether it be physical or spiritual, then aren't we denying His provision for us?"

Sara had pondered her words for a long time, and realized Catherine was right. There were many references in Scripture that taught plainly God's interest in man's everyday affairs. "But seek ye first the kingdom of God, and his righteousness; and all these things (food, drink, clothing) shall be added unto you."

Sara was able to see in Catherine, with her great wealth, a beautiful spirit, giving back to God a portion of what He had given her. She was generous, kind, loving, and lived her Christian convictions in a way that did not antagonize people but, instead, made them wonder about her source of strength and wisdom.

Sara had come to realize that peace of heart and mind came from within and had nothing to do with outward circumstances. In Catherine's mansion or in the simple crowded home of George and Lottie MacReady, she would still be God's child, and could effectively serve Him in either place.

Sara gazed at herself now in the mirror, at the high sweep of her golden hair atop her head and the delicate wisps of curls that lay along her cheeks. The skin of her neck and shoulders was smooth and white, and Sara's eyes were bright and very blue in anticipation of the day ahead. She determined to make it a happy day, for she would be seeing Dominic for the last time.

Beginning with the firing of the Christmas guns—"A custom the French settlers left us," Catherine explained—the day was filled with excitement.

The house was beautifully decorated with evergreen boughs and wild holly, and huge fires blazed in several fireplaces. There was a throng of happy guests. The children had discovered little gifts in their stockings early in the morning and were busy playing with balloons and crackling sparklers, paper horns and whistles. There were wrestling matches and shooting contests for the men, and food in abundance.

The traditional Christmas dinner was served at three o'clock and included the best hams from the smokehouse; oysters by the barrelful, shipped from coastal waters; fruitcakes and a special Martha Washington Christmas cake known as the Great Cake, made with forty eggs. Fruits and vegetables, nuts and cheeses rounded out the fare, and Sara ate more than she had planned to, and now feared she would rip the seams of her lovely dress.

"Virginians love celebrations," Dominic told her

once when they were standing together gazing at the Yule log that burned brightly in the very ballroom where they had danced the waltz together. Sara could almost hear the music, and feel Dominic's hand upon her waist. Sadly, she had been in his arms, but never in his heart. She reminded herself, on this last day they would spend together, that it would have been better never to know ecstasy at all, than to be tormented by unrequited love.

She knew he was staring at her, and she looked up into those eyes that could melt all resistance. "I'll never forget you, Dominic," she said, and then she slowly walked away to join Catherine and some of her friends.

On the day after Christmas, Sara stood at the front door of The Willows, waiting for Catherine and Lydia to come downstairs. Her belongings were neatly packed and waiting in two large valises at the side of the great hall.

"I hope the doctor is right in saying it's safe for you to leave," Dominic said with an edge in his voice.

"I'll be careful," she promised him sweetly. "No more staying out all night in the rain."

He laughed a little, but there was a hollow ring to the sound. "Sara, I hate for you to leave under these circumstances. You should have let me explain, or at least try to explain, why I am the way I am."

"I think I understand. It has to do with your sister Claudia."

"Someone told you?"

"Yes."

"I suppose it does," he said sadly.

The commotion at the top of the stairs told them Catherine and Lydia were on their way down.

"Dominic, while there is time, I want to thank you for allowing me to stay here during my recovery, and for taking such good care of me. I know I was a terrible burden. . . ."

"You were never a burden." His eyes were fierce.

But Sara knew better. Lydia had told her often enough.

"I put you to a lot of trouble." Her gaze was soft upon his face. "I'll never forget your kindness to me."

Dominic took her arm and leaned toward her. "Sara . . ." he whispered tentatively.

"Good afternoon, you two." Lydia was there, with Catherine a few steps behind. "Looks like you're ready to go, Sara," she said cheerfully, as she gave the pair a measured look.

Several slaves followed Catherine, carrying the luggage which they took through the front door to the waiting carriage.

"Dominic," Catherine said, going to him and placing a warm hand on his arm, "I don't know how to thank you for saving Sara's life and for bringing her here and caring for her so splendidly. Just look at how healthy and well she is now. You played the Good Samaritan perfectly."

"Not so perfectly, I'm afraid, for I'm losing her now. But thank you, Catherine. I was more than happy to do it for you, and for Sara, too, of course."

"We'll take good care of her and not let her do too much until the doctor says she is completely well. May I threaten her that you'll come over and deal with her if she doesn't mind doctor's orders?"

Dominic smiled and glanced at Sara. "You may. I would do so with pleasure."

"Well, you won't have the chance," Sara laughed, "because I'm going to be a very good girl." She sobered. "I've learned that problems aren't solved in running away." She looked directly into Dominic's eyes. She knew he was running away, too—from God.

A scurrying of feet along the floor turned everyone's attention to little Lizzie, frantically running toward them. Breathlessly she threw her arms around Sara's legs and clung to her. Sara reached down and scooped her up in her arms.

"Lizzie, Lizzie, how wonderful that you came to say goodbye! I so wanted to see you before I left."

The chubby black child clasped her arms around Sara's neck, nearly choking her in her exuberance.

"It's obvious she doesn't want you to go," laughed Catherine.

"Why did you ever let her grow so attached to you, Sara?" Lydia chided.

Sara nodded woefully. "I didn't mean to. Dominic warned me about that, too, but she came to my room this morning and we had the nicest visit, didn't we, Lizzie?"

The child said nothing, but continued to cling to Sara's neck, her fat little hands tightly locked so that when Dominic tried to remove them, even with his greater strength he found it difficult. Finally he set her down on the floor, and she ran away from them only to return in a moment, holding something in her hands. She offered the object to Sara. It was the music box, the very one Dominic had given her only two nights earlier.

Lydia gasped. "Dominic, isn't that your mother's music box? However did Lizzie get it?" She turned on the child. "Lizzie, you bad girl! You stole that music box, didn't you? You must be severely punished."

She reached for the child, but Sara pulled Lizzie quickly into her arms and held her tightly against her.

"I g-gave her the box, Lydia."

"What? How could you do such a thing?" Lydia fumed. "How presumptuous of you. It's not your box to give."

"Oh, but it was," Dominic said. "I gave it to Sara."

"You—what?"

"I said I gave it to her, Lydia. Do I need your permission to give a gift?"

Obviously hurt by Dominic's stinging rebuke, Lydia backed away.

"I'm sorry, Dominic," Sara apologized repentantly. "I know I shouldn't have given it to her, but when she was sitting on my bed this morning, her eye caught the box. I showed it to her and how it worked, and she played it over and over. You should have seen her! Her eyes were so big I thought they would pop right out of her head. She had obviously never seen anything so wondrous and . . . and I wanted her to have something that belonged especially to her. . . ."

"Oh, for heaven's sake, Sara!" Lydia spat out the words. "You shouldn't worry. Slave children have no feelings! She's a lucky little girl to be living here on Dominic's plantation where she's well-fed and housed and cared for."

"I know that, Lydia. Dominic—" Sara's eyes pled for forgiveness— "I don't know what to say. I gave it to Lizzie—not because it wasn't precious to me, but because it *was!*"

"She'll have it broken in a day's time," Lydia grunted. "Sara, it was a *family* heirloom."

"It was Sara's gift to do with as she saw fit," Dominic defended her. "I can understand fully why she chose to give it away." He took Lizzie from Sara and hoisted her up in his powerful arms. She went willingly to him.

"Lizzie is a dear little girl." He smiled at her. "And you're right, Sara. I'm sure she's never had anything special in her whole life—something uniquely her own."

Lizzie sat very still in his arms and he kissed the child lightly on the cheek.

"You may keep the music box, child, but please be careful with it. It belonged to a very great lady at one time, and she would want you to take good care of it for her." His voice choked with the memory.

Lizzie seemed to understand, and nodded meekly. Dominic put her down and she scurried away, but at the end of the hall she turned and waved to Sara, who felt the tears running down her cheeks as she watched the little girl disappear through a doorway.

Sara was grateful to Dominic for his kindness to Lizzie. She suspected there were many tender feelings locked up in his heart that he seldom allowed free rein. Dominic Lansford was not an easy man to know, but he was very much worth knowing. She knew she would miss him—more than she ought.

There was a knock at the door, and Dominic strode over to open it.

"Mr. Lansford, I've come to see Sara. I've just arrived in town." It was John Hamilton.

"John!" Sara exclaimed, moving toward him and extending her hands which he accepted enthusiastically. "How very good to see you."

From the corner of her eye, she noted Dominic's scowl.

Sara was never quite sure how John Hamilton became her tutor, except that it began during her first week back at Grand Oak. Since she was in the last stages of her recovery, she could be up and about, as long as she was careful to rest several times a day.

So when John daily appeared at Catherine's house, it was quite natural that they should discuss some of the things Sara wanted most to learn. Her week of recovery slipped into two, and mention of her return to the Society ceased.

Sara enjoyed learning. In fact, she reveled in it.

There was no subject which did not interest her. Catherine taught her the piano and a little about singing. John talked with her about great Americans like Patrick Henry, George Washington, and John Marshall. She learned a hundred facts about Virginia. She pondered the rule of George III of England, and the political ascendance of Napoleon Bonaparte in France. She and John examined the presidencies of John Adams and Thomas Jefferson who was just coming to the end of his first term, and dissected the government of Frederick William III of Prussia. They talked about the united England and Ireland, wondered what impact Admiral Lord Nelson would have upon the English government, studied the details behind Aaron Burr's killing Alexander Hamilton, a distant relative of John's, and Sara was overwhelmed by the purchase of the territory of Louisiana from France for fifteen thousand dollars, a sum of money she could not begin to fathom.

She tried not to imagine how much more exciting it would be if Dominic were her schoolmaster. His quick mind, vivid imagination, and dramatic ability would have brought all the facts she was learning that much more to life. But Dominic was not there, and John was, so it was John to whom she was grateful for her new knowledge.

"It won't do you any good, you know," Lydia told her, "all this frantic attempt to become civilized. It won't matter at all in the Society."

But Sara just smiled and answered that learning for learning's sake was enough reward for her.

Day followed day, and Sara was not aware that John was falling in love with her. When he finally asked her to marry him, as they were strolling at the outskirts of Charlottesville one day, she was utterly flabbergasted.

"I love you with all my heart, Sara," he admitted

ardently. "I have from the very first moment I saw you."

Sara blushed. She liked John, respected and admired him. He was a successful businessman, kind and considerate, attentive, respectful. There was no reason in the world why she shouldn't love him. But she didn't.

Looking into his eager face, seeing his eyes fondly fastened upon hers, Sara tried to think of John holding her in his arms and kissing her. The blush deepened, and Sara knew she could never feel for John what she had felt for Dominic. The excitement wasn't there. The magnetism that had drawn her to Dominic was missing. Her heart beat on in its steady pace, not wildly nor erratically. But perhaps that kind of sensation was not necessary in marriage.

She looked at John with new eyes, seeing him differently now that he had proposed. His eyes adored her. A hopeful expression raised his smooth forehead so that Sara was tempted to say yes to relieve his agony, to see the look of joy she knew would flood his countenance.

"I can tell I've shocked you with my declaration," John said gently to Sara, "and I should be whipped for doing so in a public place. You could hardly fall into my arms and agree to be my wife right here on the streets of Charlottesville, now could you, Sara?"

His imploring gaze told her that was exactly what he wished she would do.

"John," Sara laid her hand on his arm, trying to find the right words, "I'm overwhelmed by your proposal, and yes, it surprises me greatly. You and I have become good friends in the past weeks. In fact, I've taken advantage of that friendship, using up much of your time to discuss things that are common knowledge to most other people. You've been kind and patient in indulging my intense desire to learn as much as I can."

157

John placed his own hand over Sara's. She liked the warmth of his touch, although it did not send a thrill through her.

"We're good friends—" she repeated feebly.

"And that's the key, I believe," he interrupted her, "to a good and enduring marriage. Husband and wife must be more than passionate lovers; they must like each other first, as friends."

Again Sara felt the blush of embarrassment creep up her neck at the thought that they might someday be passionate lovers. Thank goodness the maidenly pink was covered by the collar of her dress, she thought.

Her mind raced to another scene of which she had been a part, not many months ago. She saw herself sitting beside Dominic in his handsome carriage. She felt his hand resting on the back of the seat and the gentle brushing of his lips upon hers. She recalled that moment in every vivid detail. There had been fire, a sudden igniting of feelings she had never experienced before. With just a gentle touch he had exploded her emotions and gathered them back to himself, and she had known in an instant that what she felt for him she was not likely to feel for another.

Sara looked down at John's hand. His touch was merely pleasant. She sighed and her eyes drifted up again to look into his eyes, and then they were diverted from his face by a sudden movement. Someone was standing nearby—someone who, she realized now, had been watching them for some time. She had only seen the silhouette of his figure in her peripheral vision and had not focused on the reality of his presence until now.

Just as John leaned down and delicately kissed her on the cheek, Sara found herself staring into the smoldering eyes of Dominic Lansford. His look sent shivers of delight through her. John Hamilton believed her shudder to be a pleasant reaction to his kiss.

158

"Sara," he murmured, even as her heart fled from her body across infinite space to the man who was observing them with scowling interest. How long had he been there? Had he overheard John's proposal of marriage?

"Take me home, John, please," Sara said, wishing herself a thousand miles away.

John cupped his hand beneath her elbow and led her back toward his carriage. He did not see Dominic, so besotted was he with what he supposed to be the encouraging response to his proposal by the woman he loved.

But Sara was uncomfortably aware of Dominic's presence. She was amazed that she wanted to run to him and throw herself into his arms. Every nerve ending she possessed was tingling with excitement, and her thoughts remained behind with the tall, dark man whom, she knew, was staring at them at that very moment. Only one black thought disturbed her euphoria; Dominic had not been, even once, to see her since she'd returned to Catherine's house. Not once.

Catherine was thrilled when she heard from Sara about John's proposal. Sara longed to confide to her how she really felt about John—and Dominic. But something held her back, though she knew Catherine would be sympathetic.

When, a few days later, Catherine announced that she was giving a twentieth birthday party for Sara, Sara instinctively knew her sister-in-law hoped it would be a time for announcing an engagement as well.

Lydia's reaction to the news of John Hamilton's proposal was merely a grunt. Characteristically, she did not even try to keep Sara from hearing her reply to her mother, "John must be daft. Sara is the worst possible wife he could choose."

She tossed her mane of magnificent red hair, and

flounced out of the room, leaving Catherine with a look of weary dismay on her face.

Lydia had become more and more antagonistic toward Sara since their return from Dominic's. The consideration she had shown while Sara was recuperating had disappeared the instant they had stepped back inside Grand Oak. Sara reluctantly concluded that Lydia's deference to her had been an act to impress Dominic, and as the day of Sara's party drew nearer, Lydia became even more sharp-tongued.

All the young people who had been at Dominic's Winter Frolic were invited to the party, and all accepted, except Dominic who sent word that he would be in Kentucky, selling some of his prize horses to a large breeder there. Sara tried not to be disappointed, but she was, and perhaps it was that very feeling that made her begin to wonder what it would be like to be married to John Hamilton, who never disappointed her.

CHAPTER 14

ON THE DAY OF HER ELEGANT BIRTHDAY DINNER, Sara found herself delighting in her many guests. She appreciated the friendship they warmly gave her and didn't at all feel like an outsider.

John's gift to her was a companion set of Shakespeare's plays. On the inside covers, he scribbled affectionate congratulations.

Jane Robertson gave her a tiny mongrel puppy who had such an adorable face that Sara kept kissing his soft wet nose.

Catherine had asked Sara that morning if she had made a decision on John's proposal of marriage, and Sara had surprised herself by saying she needed more time to think about it. Catherine's face had lighted in anticipation of the announcement she felt was imminent.

At the party when someone teased John and Sara about spending so much time together, Jane Robertson blurted out the secret Sara had shared with her. "Didn't you know? John has asked Sara to marry him!"

Screams of delight escaped from the young ladies present. The men clapped John on the back and pumped his hand, assuming that Sara had agreed to his proposal.

John was greatly embarrassed, and Sara was aghast. But Lydia was pleased, and she cleared her throat. "Before you all get too excited over the news about our dear Sara, I think you should know that she hasn't given John an answer yet. Isn't that right, Sara?"

Sara's heart was thudding in her chest. They shouldn't be discussing such a personal matter in public. She knew John was uncomfortable, and she felt additional pressure to give an affirmative answer to spare him further humiliation.

"Our proposed engagement is not open to discussion tonight, Lydia," Sara said with a sharpness intended to make Lydia drop the conversation.

But Lydia was not at all dissuaded from saying more. "Oh, but it should be, Sara. After all, don't you think John deserves to know what went wrong with your first marriage?"

"Lydia, this is none of your business," John growled, but Lydia was too determined now to stop.

"I don't know all the details, of course," she persisted sweetly, addressing the attentive guests, "but for some reason that only Sara knows, her marriage to my uncle was . . . well . . . 'incomplete'."

There were gasps of surprise from everyone, including Catherine. John stared at Sara, and she felt as though someone had hit her a hard blow in the stomach.

"That kind of rejection is devastating to a woman." Lydia continued her unrelenting exposé.

"Stop it!" Sara ordered as dizzying waves of nausea swept through her. How had Lydia discovered her secret—that had made her question her own worth, her womanliness.

She began to tremble as everyone twittered over the shocking revelation. Then Sara burst into tears, burying her face in her hands. She ran from the crowd, hearing John and Catherine call out to her, but she didn't stop until she was upstairs, locked in her room.

Because her eyes were full of tears, she bumped into a chair and cried out in pain. Groping her way to the bed, she flung herself down, weeping bitterly.

How had Lydia known? Sara had sometimes wondered if the elders in the Society had suspected that the marriage had never been consummated. If so, Simon would have had to tell them, for she never had. And she had never discussed it with Catherine, either. The only person who knew was . . . was. . . .

Sara sat up on the bed, startled with the intensity of her suspicion. It must have been Dominic! She had told him in the library of his house on Christmas Eve. It must have been he who had told Lydia.

Such a torrent of rage swept through Sara she thought she would faint. But the bitter anger soon dissolved into heartbreaking anguish. To think that now all those people downstairs knew that her husband had rejected her. The thought echoed in her mind, like the pounding of relentless surf upon a beach. Why hadn't Simon wanted her? Why? Why?

Now John would not want her as his wife, either. What man would? All those handsome young men flocking around John in sympathy would wonder what was the matter with her. Most of them had flirted with her outrageously at Dominic's Winter Frolic. Now they would be relieved they had not become more involved.

But poor John. How humiliated he must be—and she had run away and left him to face everyone alone.

Sara cried until her eyes were swollen and sore, ignoring Catherine's pleas to come in and talk with her. John, too, came to the door, begging her to let him in. But she steadfastly refused and finally ceased her sobbing.

Her life had been turned topsy-turvy—first, by Dominic; again, by Lydia. Now she knew, with greater certainty than ever before, where she belonged. Not at The Willows nor at Grand Oak—but in the Society where people were not cruel, and accepted her for herself. It was time to go back home.

CHAPTER 15

IT WAS A STRANGE DAY. The smell of spring blew fresh across the open fields, but the sky, sunny one minute, was overcast the next. Sara had taken a chance that it wouldn't rain, and had washed the MacReadys' clothes and now was laying them carefully over a long piece of rope strung between two trees to dry.

Nearby, Eva was playing contentedly on the grass. Sara could not believe how much the child had grown.

Sara's other two charges, three-year-old twins Nathaniel and Thomas, were busily examining the contents of a wooden box their father had given them in which was to be found an odd assortment of things no longer used on the farm. They were good children, energetic and curious, but obedient. Sara loved them very much. But she was not happy.

She had been back in the Society for a month. The MacReadys had, of course, asked questions about what had transpired in Virginia, and Sara had tried to answer their questions truthfully—though incompletely. For the whole truth of those months brought her such pain that her natural spontaneity and gaiety was dimmed. They would not—could not—begin to understand. The two worlds were so very different; it was best not to contemplate that other life.

But, of course, that was impossible. Sara's mind refused to rest, a relentless, continual stream of thoughts about Catherine and Grand Oak and Lydia and John parading through her consciousness.

John. She still could see his disappointed eyes and sad smile when he, a true gentleman, had assured her he understood her reasons for refusing to be his wife. She knew perfectly well he didn't understand at all. He had tried to assure her their married life would be far different. And she had believed him. John was a wonderful, loving individual. He would have made a fine husband.

But she didn't love him.

Sara sighed deeply and squinted into the bright sun as she laid a heavy black skirt over the line and fastened it in position with a wooden pin. *Love.* Love was such a strange phenomenon—so much more complex than she had ever imagined. Sara had felt quietly loved by the Society, protectively enfolded into their simple ways. Simon was another matter, of course. That he cared enough to put a roof over her head and food on her table must have been a form of loving, she mused. Yet he had remained strangely aloof and distant.

Then there was God's love which surrounded her like a divine embrace. It was gentle, supportive, strengthening.

Dominic had introduced her to yet another dimension of love, and she had not been prepared for the tempestuous emotions such passion evoked in her. Yet, God Himself had created it—had ordained it so His creatures might never be lonely, she recalled from her study of Scripture. And He had proclaimed it "good."

Finally, after weeks of analyzing her feelings,

agonizing over them, she was forced to accept the truth that surfaced above all other thoughts: she was—had been—very much in love with Dominic Lansford.

No matter how hard she tried, she could not forget the deep timbre of his voice, the strength of his hands on her arms, the playful curl of his lips when he was amused.

Somehow the bad times with Dominic were losing their reality. When she recalled his anger and disgust, the brutal words seemed softer now. They didn't cut through her as sharply.

Her heart always beat rapidly whenever she thought of him. Though she wished it to be still, its very thumping told her she would never feel for any man what she had felt for Dominic, in that faraway world she would never see again.

The warm sun on her face felt good. She bent down into the wooden bucket for another piece of clothing and shook it to straighten out the wrinkles before placing it on the rope.

She looked up, startled. Something stood between her vision and the white blinding sphere of the sun as it fanned out across the sky. She could not at first make out the dark figure. Then it moved closer and she saw that it was a man on horseback. Slowly horse and rider approached, and she stood, holding the wet cloth in her hands, trying to focus her eyes so she could tell who was visiting the MacReadys so early in the morning.

The greeting she was about to call out stuck in her throat as she recognized the face, the figure, the eyes.

"Hello, Sara."

The voice struck her like a slap across her face. She saw the dark eyes, the thick hair, the familiar hands holding lightly the reins of the magnificent animal upon which he rode.

"Dominic?"

The question was rhetorical, for she recognized him only too well. But it couldn't be he! her heart screamed in denial. He lived hundreds of miles away, in another state, in another life that she had tasted but was no longer a part of. How could he be here?

"Am I welcome?"

Sara dropped the wet bodice into the basket and began to wipe her hands on the sturdy gray apron that covered the front of her black dress.

"Of course."

He dismounted, the muscles of his legs bulging beneath the tight pants he wore. He stayed beside the horse, a little distance from Sara.

"How are you?" he asked, looking directly at her with that penetrating gaze that had kept her awake and her mind whirling for the past weeks she had been separated from him.

"I'm fine," she lied. Her emotions were being shredded with wild rushings to and fro, but she was fine, she told herself. "I'm just fine," she repeated.

"Good."

There was an awkward silence. Sara looked down at her hands, knotted together so tightly they were white.

Dominic shifted from one leg to the other and looked out over the land. "This is beautiful country."

"Yes."

"It's greener than I thought it would be."

"The soil is rich. There's an abundance of flowers, and it's perfect for farming. We grow hay and oats, potatoes and apples."

"I see."

"There is also fine grazing for cattle."

"I'd thought there would be."

Sara made the mistake of looking straight into Dominic's eyes, and when she found him staring at her intently, her mouth went dry and her hands fell to her sides. She wanted to look away, but found she couldn't. She had never been able to resist Dominic's intense scrutiny, and it rested on her now and forced her to return his look.

"Sara, would you take me around? I'd like to see the farms, and meet the people, too, if you could introduce me."

Was he here on business then? she wondered.

A part of Sara instantly responded to the invitation—anything to be with him one moment longer—but her reason dictated otherwise. She wanted him to go away so she could try to forget him and everything that had happened between them. Her heart told her one thing; her mind, another.

"Let's go into the house," she suggested.

She called the boys to her and propelled them forward as she settled Eva on her hip. Dominic picked up the basket of washing, without being asked, and followed Sara toward the humble dwelling she shared with the MacReadys.

Inside, Mrs. MacReady was standing in front of a large fireplace that dominated the simple room, stirring a heavy iron pot, from which drifted a delicious odor. A teen-aged girl was cutting potatoes on a sturdy wooden table, the knife, sharp and swift. A younger girl, in the same gray dress and apron that her mother and sister wore, was tugging at some yarn, trying to straighten it out, though it resisted her efforts.

At the sound of the door opening, the girls looked up, and Mrs. MacReady turned around, but she never stopped her stirring, even when she saw the tall handsome stranger with Sara.

"Sara," she acknowledged the girl's presence.

"Lottie, there's someone I'd like you to meet."

Dominic set the laundry down, then followed Sara over to the fire, glancing around the room as he did so, his eyes taking in the rough-hewn floor, the sturdy and simple wooden table and chairs, the windows of paper soaked in linseed oil, the bare walls.

Did he find the room cozy and full of love, as Sara did, or was he repulsed by its austerity? she wondered.

"This is Dominic Lansford—from Virginia."

Lottie smiled, not at all self-conscious about the large gap in her smile. A horse had knocked out the tooth when she was thirteen.

"Mr. Lansford," Lottie said.

"Dominic, this is Lottie MacReady," Sara went on nervously, "the mother of these children, and a few who aren't here at the moment. She's also my friend."

"How do you do, madame?" The richness of his voice and charm of manner made Lottie MacReady eye him with curiosity.

"I was riding through," he said, "on business, and heard that there might be some good horses for sale in this valley."

"Oh?" Lottie questioned. "Then you were misinformed. We're only farmers here, and need all the horses we have for plowin'. You look like a gentleman breeder. Doubt that our animals would be the kind 'twould interest you."

"You're right, Lottie," Sara said. "Mr. Lansford raises fine quarter horses in Virginia."

"Well, like I said, he won't find any breedin' stock around here."

"He asked if I could show him the valley. Would that be all right? I won't stay away long. I'll finish the washing first. . . ."

"Nonsense. Ruth can do it. You go on and show Mr. Lansford what he wants to see."

Dominic looked over at the girls, both of whom were gaping at him and becoming giggly at his attention. The older one muttered, *"Anner satt leit."*

Dominic glanced at Sara for an explanation, but she gave none.

"Thank you, madame," Dominic said then, bowing slightly at the waist. "I appreciate your allowing Sara to accompany me. You needn't worry about her safety. I knew her well in Virginia. We're good friends."

"I see." But she didn't see, since Sara had never mentioned knowing the handsome and sophisticated Mr. Lansford.

Dominic tethered his horse more securely to a tree and then he and Sara began their walk. The sun had disappeared, but it was still warm out. Humid. It felt like rain was on the way.

The farms were laid out in neat multiple-acre parcels, some larger than others, depending on the size of a man's family and ability to work it. That they were prosperous farms, and well taken care of, was evident. Sara explained that beets, plums, green beans, cabbage, tomatoes, and corn were some of the crops raised there. There were also lots of children, of all ages.

"A man works hard to build a successful farm—for his sons," Sara said.

"And what of his daughters?"

"Hopefully they will marry within the Society so the families will remain close."

"As you did."

"Yes."

"Everyone wears similar clothing," Dominic commented, observing that the men and boys wore black pants, blue shirts, and black hats, while the girls and women had on dark dresses and long aprons, their hair pulled back under little white caps or dark bonnets.

"We think there is virtue in being plain, both in our dress and in our homes."

"Is that what God requires of everyone who wants to be His humble servant?"

Sara glanced up at him, surprised that there was no derision in his voice. "I . . . I used to think so, until I met Catherine. She enlightened me in many ways, taught me new truths."

"Including, I hope, the Bible verse that teaches that man looks on the outward appearance, but God judges the heart."

Their eyes met, and held.

"Yes," she answered barely above a whisper.

They continued their walk, while Sara tried to sort out what was different about Dominic. He had changed.

Despite their somber dress, the members of the Society were a happy people, and adults and children alike smiled in a friendly manner when Sara introduced them to Dominic. Had he been a stranger, they would have been more reticent, but as Sara's friend, he was readily accepted. Dominic's graciousness was genuine and puzzled Sara more than a little, knowing how he felt about the group.

The men answered his questions forthrightly. They discussed with him cattle and crops and horses, and even foreign trade. And Dominic found something to say to the women about their children or homes. They sensed it was not idle flattery, but sincere interest.

After they left Elder Johns' farm, Dominic commented, "I'm very impressed with the people here, Sara. Even though they don't know it, I owe them an apology."

"Really? Why?"

"Because in my ignorance I thought they were isolationists, that they wanted only to live their own lives and not be bothered about the rest of the world. I believed that they were content to let others secure their freedom and right to privacy, while they merely enjoyed these benefits without contributing anything

172

toward their attainment. But I see now that I was wrong. The men are very aware of what is going on throughout this country and the rest of the world. They're wise farmers and astute businessmen. I just wish they had horses here. I'd feel very safe in dealing with them."

They moved on as threatening clouds gathered overhead. Sara failed to notice them or the fact that the air had grown chilly. In Dominic's presence she felt a warmth that required no sun. She didn't care why he was there. The fact that they were together, if only for a few moments, was all she wanted. She would sort out the reasons for it later, after he had gone.

"What did the young girl say back at the house?" Dominic asked Sara. They had by now walked a long way from the MacReadys.

Sara smiled. "She was repeating what children learn very early in the Society that *unser satt leit*, our sort of people, are different from *anner satt leit*, the other sort of people."

Dominic grinned. "So I'm the other sort of people?"

"Yes."

He stopped and leaned against a thick tree. "I like it here," he said decidedly. "There's a simplicity of life that binds you together, and by helping each other, you help yourselves as well."

Sara nodded, surprised by his perception of her way of life.

"The people are gracious, and have a sense of humor," he went on.

"Oh, yes. While we're serious, we don't take ourselves too seriously. Does that make sense?"

"Certainly."

Dominic made a sweeping gesture that encompassed the entire valley. "I can see why you feel safe here, Sara. And content. This way of life answers those questions most people struggle with. What shall I do with my life? Does anyone care about me? Who shares my values? Who will take care of me if trouble comes? Who desires the best for me?" There was a strange glow of appreciation in his eyes when he looked at her. "It's all here."

A gust of wind whipped at the skirt of Sara's dress, and she shivered. Dominic looked up.

"It's going to rain. We'd better get back."

Thunder rolled across the sky. They turned around and walked quickly.

"The place where my sister is living, in Ohio, is very similar to the Society. At the time I went there, I was too blinded by prejudice to appreciate its virtues or even to see it as it really was. A lot of misery might have been avoided had I been wiser."

He looked down and saw Sara's surprised expression.

"I've come to terms with many things since you left, Sara. I want to thank you."

"For what?"

"For showing me that there's a lot more to life than raising fine horses. And that being cynical and negative is a ridiculous waste of energy."

His velvet smooth words and his eyes, with a new and deeper look, gathered Sara's heart to him. "You spoke softly of your faith, and I refused to listen. But when you were gone, I heard the words again. I've come back, Sara—to God," he said. Her soft exclamation caused him to chuckle lightly. "God loves even me, Sara, as much as I tried to ignore that fact. But no more. I'm a new creature in Christ Jesus, as the Good Book says."

"Oh, Dominic, I'm so happy for you!" Sara's eyes sparkled with delight. She could see that he was a new man. She could see it in his face. How obvious it was that he was a new person. She could see it in his eyes,

sense it in his manner, hear it in his voice. Had he
ridden all the way from Virginia to tell her so?

Dominic looked up. "It's starting to sprinkle." He
scowled at the miles of dark foreboding clouds that
tumbled across the vast and ominous sky. "Where's
the nearest house?"

"Let's try to get back to the MacReadys'."

A tumultuous roar of thunder was followed by rain
that fell heavily. Their clothes were soaked in a matter
of seconds.

"The Talbots' place is just down the road," Sara
changed her mind as they started running. "But
they're. . . ."

"Let's go. You remember what happened to you
the last time you were out in the rain."

She did indeed.

Sara had trouble keeping up with Dominic's fast
pace. After some minutes a small square building
appeared.

"Is that it?" Dominic yelled into the fierce wind.

"Yes, but. . . ." And then Sara stumbled, sprawling flat out on the muddy road. Her face hit the
ground and she cried out as pain raced through her
cheeks and forehead. She found herself being gathered into Dominic's strong arms and lifted as easily as a
child. Her head rested on his shoulder, and she lay
still as he charged on to the Talbot place which was
little more than a shack.

"I hope they don't mind sudden company," Dominic sputtered above the storm. He reached the door
and kicked it open with his booted foot. With a violent
shudder, it flew back and hit the inside wall. Dominic
strode inside and stopped abruptly.

"What's this?" he said, puzzled.

The room was completely dark. There was no sign
of life. He put Sara down.

"I tried to tell you," she began, looking ruefully
back at the door with its splintered hinges that would

175

need to be repaired, "the Talbots aren't here. Mrs. Talbot's aunt, who was very dear to her, died in the next county, and the entire family went for the burying. I heard they won't be back for another week."

"Well," Dominic said, going back to the door and closing it as best he could, "then we're alone."

Across the darkness of the room Sara could feel his eyes on her, and she felt a sudden panic.

"The first thing we have to do," he said decisively, "is to get you out of those wet clothes."

CHAPTER 16

SARA'S HANDS FLEW INSTINCTIVELY to her throat as Dominic whirled her around and began unfastening the cloth hooks down the back of her dress.

"What are you doing?" she gasped, so taken aback that she stood there dumbly.

"I have no intention of letting you catch pneumonia again." When his cold, wet fingers touched the sensitive skin at the nape of her neck, Sara pulled away from him, clutching the bodice of her dress with both hands.

"I can't allow you to do this!"

"Don't be ridiculous, Sara. I mean you no harm. On the contrary, I'm trying to save your life."

Dominic looked furtively around the room, then strode to one end where he grabbed a blanket from the foot of a bed and carried it back to Sara. "Take your own clothes off, then, but do it! Then cover yourself up in this while I make a fire."

Sara stumbled backward into a dark corner, clutching the blanket to her body.

With cold and nervous hands, she fumbled to strip

away the wet garments that stubbornly clung to her damp body. Dominic kept his back discreetly turned and continued to arrange the wood in the fireplace.

Finishing the task, Sara scooped the blanket up and wrapped it tightly around her. For a moment she watched Dominic as he diligently worked with flint and steel to ignite the wood shavings beneath the long and sturdy logs that Mr. Talbot, an orderly man, had left ready for use. The muscles in Dominic's back rose and fell as he concentrated on his task, and Sara admired the broadness of his shoulders and the power that she knew lay within them.

Soon the flames were licking the good dry wood and sending heat and a delicious woodsy scent into the room. Dominic turned around and saw Sara standing in the darkness.

"Come over here where it's warm," he ordered. "You must get warm as quickly as possible."

Sara obeyed.

Dominic took a cloth she had seen him hold outside in the rain and began gently to wipe the dirt from her face. "Are you hurt?" he asked softly.

"N . . . no," she said, avoiding his eyes, scarcely able to breathe. "My clothes . . ." she gestured toward the bed.

"I'll take care of them."

The thought of Dominic's laying out her clothes to dry sent a wave of embarrassment through Sara. She turned back, determined to attend to the matter herself. But Dominic's hand tightened on her shoulder.

"Sara, this is hardly the time to be maidenly. I had, after all, a mother and a sister. I know about women's clothing."

Dominic left Sara for a moment and went back to the bed which stood against the wall. Hastily he yanked another blanket from it and brought it over to

178

the fireplace where he arranged it on the floor, over the braided rug.

"Here, sit on this. I want you as close to the warmth as you can get."

He helped her settle herself, then went to attend to her wet clothing. She heard him shaking them out before bringing them back to the fire, where he laid them over a straight chair, pulled just close enough to the heat to dry the garments without singeing them. Sara watched him, fascinated by the ease and dexterity of his movements. Then pulling the heavy wooden table closer to the fire, Dominic finally dropped his long frame to the floor and leaned back against one sturdy leg, facing Sara, too near for her comfort.

Beads of water clotted his thick dark hair and there was still rain on his face. Instinctively, before she thought about what she was doing, Sara reached up and brushed away some of the water from his cheeks.

He grabbed her hand and held the palm against his lips in an impetuous gesture. Her heart almost stopped beating. She could not look away, even when he raised his eyes and gazed at her for a very long time.

Then, reluctantly it seemed, he released her hand and stared into the fire.

"I'm sorry I wasn't able to be at your birthday party. Catherine told me you were more beautiful than ever."

"It was a nice party."

"Until the end—when Lydia made her little speech about your marriage to Simon."

Sara shot him an angry look. She was surprised that it still bothered her, but she had not forgotten the humiliation.

"Did Catherine tell you about it?"

"Yes. How do you suppose Lydia found out?"

Sara glared at him. "There was only one way, Dominic. You!"

He looked genuinely surprised. "I said nothing to Lydia about your marriage, Sara. You must believe me."

A spark of resentment flashed in Sara's eyes, then disappeared. "It doesn't matter any more. It's over."

Dominic leaned toward her, his manner tense. "It matters to me, Sara. I would never have betrayed you. Lydia must have overheard us."

She studied him for a moment and sighed. "I believe you, Dominic."

He settled back and kept silent for long moments. Then he said softly, "Why did you decide not to marry John Hamilton?"

"I didn't love him," Sara answered truthfully, but more quickly than was seemly, she thought, regretting her haste.

Dominic glanced at her. "Does that matter to you now? Love?"

Sara's breath caught in her throat. She didn't want to answer that question. She had made enough mistakes with Dominic. She wasn't going to admit now that she loved him. It was too late. But her senses were unusually acute, and the fact that he was so close to her caused her heart to flutter peculiarly.

"I'll never forget the first time I saw you," he said, without waiting for an answer to his question. "You were sitting in the parlor at Catherine's house, reading the Bible." He sighed. "You were so very beautiful you took my breath away. But the Book you were reading turned my heart to stone. All I could see at that moment was my sister Claudia, sitting exactly as you were sitting, studying those same Scriptures I ignorantly blamed for having taken her from us. And so began the terrible battle that raged within me every day you were there.

"I was drawn to you, Sara, to your natural beauty, to your captivating innocence, to your loveliness of character that reached out to others."

180

He turned and gazed tenderly at her, and Sara was shocked. "Every day I fell more and more in love with you, and every day I fought my feelings for you with all the determination I could muster."

He smiled faintly at Sara's amazement. "There's more, Sara. Much more."

He reached out and with one finger lightly traced an imaginary line across her cheek, as though afraid he might mar the satin skin that now was flushed to a rosy hue.

"I turned to Lydia in a vain attempt to rid myself of you, yet you lingered in my thoughts. I'm afraid I used Lydia badly and made her think I was interested in her." He shook his head sadly. "What a fool I was."

His dark eyes were moist with deep emotion as he gazed longingly into Sara's eyes, then allowed that gaze to wander down the slender column of her throat.

"Lydia told me you were going to marry her," Sara somehow managed to say.

"Never once did I give her that much encouragement. I couldn't. My heart was dead to anyone but you. Oh, Sara," Dominic's voice broke, "I treated you spitefully in a valiant attempt to keep you from rendering me helpless. Because you were so caught up in your faith and in being loyal to the Society, I was afraid there was no place for me in your life. Yet it was that very faith and loyalty that I admired most about you."

He leaned closer to her. "And because of you, Sara, I am now reconciled to God. I'm at peace with Him."

"Oh, Dominic, I'm so glad!" Her eyes shone like glistening sapphires. Dominic's confession of love for her—and now for God—was almost more than she could comprehend. Her eyes took in every precious feature of his handsome face as she felt his hands enfold her and draw her slowly to him.

"Sara, I have loved you for so very long." Slowly he lowered his head and took her lips in the gentlest of kisses, as though she were made of fine porcelain, breakable with all but the lightest of touch. His mouth was sweet upon hers. "Dearest Sara," he whispered, "will you marry me and make me the happiest of all men?"

Sara's mouth fell open and she stared at Dominic with wonder and disbelief. Had he actually asked her to marry him? Her eyes searched out every facet of his rugged face, every tiny line that drifted from his mouth and eyes. She adored him with every fiber of her being. She wanted to say yes, to scream her answer at the top of her lungs until everyone in the Society would know that she, Sara Parsons, was going to marry Dominic Lansford. But she couldn't do that. It was impossible.

She dropped her eyes to the worn blanket she was sitting on. She couldn't look at Dominic because tears blurred her vision.

"I cannot marry you, Dominic."

"Why not?"

A tremendous crack of thunder broke the eerie silence that had been punctuated only by the sounds of rain falling heavily upon the roof and the fire spitting in the hearth.

"I'm not good enough for you," she answered softly, still not looking at him. "You deserve to have a high-born lady for a wife, someone who is used to your ways—someone you can be proud of."

"Is that what you really think?"

"Yes."

"Lydia thought so, too."

Sara's eyes shot to Dominic's face. "Lydia?"

"Yes. When I came back from Kentucky, I went immediately to Grand Oak. I had to see you. Make sure you were all right. When Catherine told me you had returned to the Society, I was furious. I hadn't thought you would really go back. That I'd lose you. I realized then how very much I loved you. I told Catherine and Lydia that I was going to find you and bring you back and make you my wife."

"Lydia approved, of course."

Dominic laughed at Sara's wry comment. "Not quite. She told me you had wanted to marry me from the start, but only because of my money and my position."

Sara sat up straight. "How could she say such a despicable thing?"

"Catherine defended you vigorously. Then Lydia said you had used John Hamilton to make me jealous."

Sara groaned.

"I was jealous, you know, after I heard he was spending a great deal of time at Grand Oak, and I feared that you were beginning to care for him. I became like a wounded lion, irritable and unreasonable. People avoided me. I hadn't accepted the fact that it was my love for you that was changing my life. Lydia tried one more thing in her arsenal—she reminded me that you were low-born. That no one knew your parentage."

Sara sighed, her eyes filled with anguish. "In that, she is right. I do not know who my parents were . . . I am not worthy of you."

"Ah, Sara, how little you know of the man I have become," he sighed. "My dearest, you are God's child, His own dear daughter. What greater heritage could you wish? No matter that you cannot trace a few years of family history.

"There is nobility in every step you take; compassion and kindness in your conduct; peace and serenity in your countenance. You are a blessing, Sara my love," he paused, his eyes misting, "and it is I who

183

am unworthy of *you* . . . And I told Lydia so. Then, Catherine shocked us both with a secret she has kept for twenty years. Lydia is really the daughter of your deceased husband, Simon.''

"What!"

"It seems that many years ago Catherine had a special friend who was in love with Simon. When the girl knew she was with child and Simon refused to marry her, he and Catherine quarrelled bitterly. That's when he ran away. Catherine's friend died in childbirth, and Catherine and Andrew kept the baby and raised her as their own. They called her Lydia, which was her mother's name."

Sara covered her mouth with a trembling hand. She couldn't believe what she was hearing.

"When Lydia was four years old, Catherine heard from Simon. He was living with the Society and told her he was happy. He told Catherine never to contact him, but she wrote him a letter telling him about his child. She never heard from him again—knew nothing until the elders of the Society contacted her at the time of his death. They had found Catherine's letter among Simon's belongings."

Sara shook her head distractedly. "Lydia must have been devastated when she learned this news."

"Hysterical."

"I'm sorry—so sorry. Poor Lydia."

"When I heard that story, Sara, I knew why Simon had never touched you all those months you were married." He reached for her hand.

"Lydia's mother and Simon's wife both died in childbirth. Because he loved you, Sara, in his own way, he didn't want to risk bringing about your death, too."

Sara's eyes grew round as she saw the logic of Dominic's theory.

"My darling," Dominic kissed her hand, "please

believe me. You are a precious treasure—too rare to lose.''

Sara began to cry gently. "I was haunted by not knowing what terrible thing I had done, or what was so horribly wrong with me that Simon didn't want me.''

"And then I treated you badly, too," he chastised himself.

"I was sure you despised me, once I learned from Jane Robertson that a proper lady does not welcome a man's lovemaking. I was so ashamed that I had allowed you to hold me and kiss me."

"I shall seal Jane Robertson's mouth when I see her again! She has caused us enough trouble with her silly suppositions. What man would not want the woman of his choice to respond to him? You, my dear, in your innocence, did just that, and in so doing you turned my world upside down. You were not pretending or leading me on because of who I was or what you wanted from me. Your purity tortured me day and night as I fought to keep from falling in love with you."

He sighed happily. "But it didn't work. Nothing I did could erase the memory of your sweet softness, your warm breath caressing my face, your heart beating in rhythm with mine. You totally captivated me, without even realizing you were doing so."

His eyes became serious, his expression almost grim. "Sara, can you leave the Society, leave these people who are your family and friends, and come back with me to The Willows to be my wife?"

Her eyes searched his face and saw hope and doubt mingled there. Still carefully holding the blanket around her, Sara sighed pitifully.

"I love the Society and its ways. This has been my home all my life, Dominic."

He took in a sharp breath, and a frown creased his brow at her words. But then she laughed and her smile, so radiant, so loving, exploded over him. "But how can I do otherwise," she exclaimed, "since I have fallen as hopelessly in love with you as any woman could? I thought of you constantly when I was at Catherine's. I relived each moment we spent together, and prayed that God would forgive me for savoring the memories of your kisses. Even after I thought that what I was doing was wrong, I couldn't stop my longings for you from flooding my mind every moment of every day. . . and if you're very sure you want me, I will be honored to be your wife."

"If I'm sure . . . ?" The words floated in the air between them before his mouth crushed hers. When at last he lifted his head, he said, "A carriage with three of my people will be here tomorrow, including Delia to act as our chaperone. Can you be ready to go that soon?"

Sara gave him a playful grin. "Were you so sure you could persuade me to leave here and become your wife?"

"One way or the other, Sara Parsons, either willingly or by force, you were going to return to Virginia with me. The games of pretending were over." He kissed her lightly again. "I even threw in a large gunny sack, in case you gave me trouble. . . . But we must get back to the MacReadys," he sobered. "I don't want anything to sully your reputation with the Society, Sara."

Sara nodded, then cocked her head. "I think the rain has stopped." She ran to the door and threw it open. The air was sweet and fresh. "The sun will be out soon," she told him, smiling back across her shoulder.

He came to her, putting his arms around her waist and pulling her back against him. "The sun is already out, my darling, in my heart." He turned her around and kissed her long and with great tenderness. "I'll do everything in my power to make you happy—to give you all that you so richly deserve."

"There is only one thing more I could possibly desire, Dominic," she blushed rosily. "Will we have children?"

He smiled. "Many sons and daughters, Sara. And little Lizzie can be their companion."

"Oh yes, Dominic!" she responded joyously. "And I can teach her to read and to learn all the wondrous things I'm only now discovering! *All* children must know of God's love, Dominic—and how to think and to reason and. . . ."

"Hush, my love." He silenced her words with his lips. "There will be time for all of that . . . the rest of our lives."

ABOUT THE AUTHOR

When KATHLEEN YAPP had a glamorous career as executive secretary to the president of a major automobile corporation, and four children living at home, she had to get up as early as three o'clock in the morning to find time to write.

Now, she and her husband, Ken, a former fire fighter in the Los Angeles area, are "retired" and living in the beautiful state of Georgia, the children are grown and away, and Kathleen's dream of writing full-time is a reality. Still, she rises before 5 a.m. and goes to her computer to put down the words that become the stories she loves to tell.

Kathleen and Ken enjoy traveling, reading, fishing, and taking an active part in church and community activities. Kathleen teaches Bible classes, is a vocal soloist, and plays the piano and organ for Sunday services.

In addition, you may have seen her on national television performing the national anthem at professional baseball, basketball, and hockey games, which she's done over seventy-five times for teams in California and Georgia.

A published author of seven novels and hundreds of magazine articles and stories, Kathleen wants to be an encourager, communicating the power of God's love and enabling through all the gifts at her disposal.

"He is everything to me," she says.

Forever Classics are inspirational romances designed to bring you a joyful, heart-lifting reading experience. If you would like more information about joining our *Forever Classics* book series, please write to us:

Guideposts Customer Service
39 Seminary Hill Road
Carmel, NY 10512

Forever Classics are chosen by the same staff that prepares *Guideposts*, a monthly magazine filled with true stories of people's adventures in faith. *Guideposts* is not sold on the newsstand. It's available by subscription only. And subscribing is easy. Write to the address above and you can begin reading *Guideposts* soon. When you subscribe, each month you can count on receiving exciting new evidence of God's Presence, His Guidance and His limitless love for all of us.